Books by Charlotte MacLeod

King Devil
We Dare Not Go A 'Hunting
Cirak's Daughter
Maid of Honor

Maid of Honor

Charlotte MacLeod

ATHENEUM • 1 9 8 4 • NEW YORK

LIBRARY OF CONGRESS CATALOGING IN PUBLICATION DATA

MacLeod, Charlotte.   Maid of honor.

SUMMARY: *Fed up with her family's preoccupation with
her sister's upcoming wedding, Persis tells no one of her
music school scholarship until the disappearance of a
valuable wedding gift precipitates a crisis that reveals
a new side to her family.*
[1. Family life—Fiction]   I. Title.
PZ7.M22494Mai   1984   [Fic]   83–15653
ISBN 0–689–31019–6

Published simultaneously in Canada by
McClelland & Stewart, Ltd.
Composition by Service Typesetters, Austin, Texas
Printed and bound by Fairfield Graphics,
Fairfield, Pennsylvania
Designed by Mary Ahern
First Edition

Maid of Honor

Chapter 1

"I hate it."

Persis Green, sixteen years old and fit to be tied, scowled at her image in the bridal shop's three-way mirror. The tall, lanky reflection wearing the too-sweet, too-fluffy, totally unbecoming pale mauve gown scowled back at her. The designer sighed.

"It's all that long, dark hair. Totally ruins the effect. She'll have to cut it."

"You tell her. I've been trying for months."

Muriel Green's face swam into the mirror behind her daughter's, pinched and wan under the fluorescent lights. She'd done her best with carefully applied make-up and a well-glued hairdo, but at this point they weren't helping much. She looked just like any middle-aged woman whose feet were killing her, Persis thought. Not like somebody's mother.

Not like Persis Green's mother, anyway. Persis had always known her mother couldn't stand her. Muriel Green preferred daughters to be curly and blonde, pretty and bendable, engaged to presentable young men whose fathers had thriving businesses for them to step into. This wedding was more her idea than Loni's, and certainly more than Chet Cowles's. She'd had Chet roped and hog-tied before he'd known what hit him.

Not that Chet would know anyway, Persis thought sourly. If her future brother-in-law ever had a thought of his own, he kept it well hidden behind that pasted-on smile of his. Aside from passably good looks, an excellent barber, and his family's money, that smile was about all Chet had going for him. No wonder he didn't dare turn it off.

Loni was a smiler, too, but she wasn't smiling now. She wasn't frowning because frowns made wrinkles, and wrinkles weren't pretty. She'd simply let her face go blank. Like her mind. Persis writhed as Miss Liss jabbed in a pin and grazed her hip. Her big sister Loni's maid of honor, she was supposed to be. Some honor.

"I'm not cutting my hair," she snarled.

"Persis, you'll do as you're told and that's that," her mother snapped back. "I've already made an appointment for you at six o'clock with Antoine."

At six? You mean six *tonight*? Mama, are you crazy? It's after five already, and my recital starts at half-past seven. I ought to be back at the house getting dressed right now."

"You won't have time for that. We'll stop on the way to the hairdresser's and pick you up a sandwich. Antoine doesn't have another appointment open all this week. He's working you in as a special favor to me. And I'm not going to argue any more, so you needn't start."

4

No, she needn't. There'd been too many fights over her hair already. Down deep, Persis had known from the moment she'd seen the designs for the bridal party's gowns that she was fighting a losing battle. Okay, so a heavy, waist-length mane of almost-black hair didn't go with masses of yucky mauve ruffles. She loved it. Her hair was the only thing about her looks she did like, except her hands.

Her hands weren't pretty. They were too big and strong, and their nails had to be kept filed short so they wouldn't get in the way when she played the piano. But when she poised them over the keyboard and crashed down into the first chord of a concerto, or sent the fingers trilling and dancing into a fugue, they always took her where she wanted to go, into a world where there weren't any nagging mothers or whining sisters or stupid future brothers-in-law, or anything but herself and her music.

That was the big thing, the one thing nobody could take away from her. What if she did have to lose her hair tonight? It would grow back sooner or later. At least they couldn't cut off her hands or she wouldn't be able to carry her ladylike bouquet of purple silk pansies and baby's breath down the aisle in front of Loni.

Persis snickered at the notion. Her mother eyed her suspiciously but didn't say anything more, except to nag the harassed Miss Liss about a little pucker in the back seam.

By the time they escaped from the bridal shop, it was too late to stop for anything to eat. Persis had to be rushed straight to the hairdresser's, to have her head shoved into a sink, to be scrubbed by an assistant who was in a hurry to get out of there and didn't give a rap how hard a customer's hair got pulled. Persis had to sit still and try not to yell when the comb raked through the wet snarls. Then she had to brace herself for whatever tortures Antoine chose to dish out.

She decided the best way to survive the haircut was to shut her eyes and keep them shut. She sat there like a wooden doll, pretending to ignore the chatter between her mother and the hairdresser. At least Loni wasn't with them any longer. The bride-to-be had gone home to polish her diamond for the fourth time that day, or gab on the phone about nothing with her bridesmaids, or write thank-you notes for wedding presents her mother had already lugged back to the stores they'd come from and exchanged for something else. Loni had liked some of the original gifts better than their replacements, but she hadn't got to keep them because Mama always knew best.

As soon as the hair had been snipped beyond redemption and the weary assistant had swept it into oblivion with a long-handled floor brush, Muriel Green got up from the canvas director's chair she'd been sitting in. She handed Antoine a large bill and Persis a small one out of her alligator skin wallet. Then she put the wallet back in her Italian leather pocketbook and fastened the clasp.

"I have to run now, Persis. Grab yourself a sandwich at the delicatessen and go straight to the recital hall."

"But, Mama, what about my gown? I can't go on stage in blue jeans."

"I should hope not. Good heavens, is there no end to the bother? Why didn't you have sense enough to bring it with you?"

"How was I to know you'd made this dumb appointment? You said to meet you straight from school at the bridal shop."

"You always have an answer, don't you? All right, then. I'll send it over to the auditorium in a taxi as soon as I get home."

Before any of her previous recitals, Muriel Green would have been swamping Persis with attention: helping her dress, brushing her hair, driving her crazy about had she got her music and did she know her piece; rounding up the grandparents, goading Daddy into skipping his usual evening nap in front of the television so they could get there early and grab the best seats. This year, the one time it really mattered, Mama hardly seemd to know the recital was happening. The grandparents weren't coming. Loni couldn't be bothered. Charles Green had only grunted when Persis reminded him. Everybody was so wrapped up in this stupid wedding they couldn't think of anything else. It wasn't fair.

"Why can't you bring the dress yourself?" Persis

demanded. "What if the cab driver goes to the wrong place? What if somebody—"

"Persis, that will do. Nothing's going to happen to your dress. I'll come when I can. Good night, Antoine. Thank you again for being so marvelous with this bothersome daughter of mine. I can't tell you how much I appreciate your sparing us the time."

Big deal! Antoine was getting paid for it, wasn't he? And no doubt Mama'd given him a tip that would choke a horse on top of that. And for what? Making her hideous instead of plain ugly.

Persis knew she'd have to open her eyes sooner or later. She postponed the awful moment until Antoine, after interminable fussings and snippings, dusted off the back of her neck, flipped the protective cape away from her shoulders, and said, "Violà, mam'selle. 'Ow you like eet?"

"Your French accent's even worse than mine," she told him politely, and faced the mirror. "Oh, my God! I'm going to be sick."

Antoine spun around in alarm. Looking for a bucket, no doubt. Persis grabbed her jacket and fled so he wouldn't see the tears running down her cheeks.

Miss Folliott, her piano teacher, had hired the Community Arts Auditorium for the recital. Persis knew where it was, of course; she'd performed there often. She ran all the way, fighting back sobs, forgetting to stop and buy herself something to eat. She couldn't have choked down food, anyway. She didn't stop running until she'd reached the dressing room with its familiar smell of makeup and sweat and dancers' feet.

In a little while, the room would be full of nervous piano students getting the shine taken off their faces with wads of cotton dipped in powder, the nervous pallor touched up with dabs of rouge. Right now, Persis had the place to herself. She took advantage of this brief privacy to treat herself to a good, wet, sniffly bawl.

The crying fit relieved her overstrung nerves a little, but it left her usually clear complexion blotched with red. Who cared? She couldn't look any worse than she did already, with her hair all chopped off except a few chewed-looking tufts. And what had she done with her music? Left it home on the piano, and forgotten to tell her mother to send it along with the gown. Now she really was going to be sick.

No, she wasn't. She couldn't. She hadn't eaten anything to be sick with. Maybe that awful churning in her stomach was only hunger. Did she have time to run back out for that sandwich?

Not a chance. Persis could hear voices coming along the corridor from the stage door. One of them was Miss Folliott's, sounding as if she was already beginning to fray at the edges. She always fell apart in front of a live audience; that was why she taught instead of performing. There were a couple of jittery parents, telling their kids not to be nervous. There were the kids' voices squeaking back that they weren't, and not convincing anybody, least of all themselves.

Then there was a new man's voice saying something Persis didn't catch, and Miss Folliott answering,

"I don't know. Give it to me. I'll see if I can find— oh, Persis, there you are. Is this your dress? A cab just brought it. I had to tip the driver a dollar," she added pointedly.

"Oh, just a second." Persis fished in her jeans pocket, found the money she now wished she'd spent on supper, and handed over a dollar of it to her teacher.

Miss Folliott held out the long, slithery garment bag. "Here, you'd better take it by the hanger so it won't get wrinkled."

"Thanks. I got hung up over a fitting for that crummy wedding of my sister's and didn't have time to go home and change. My mother said she'd. . . ."

Persis's voice died. She'd spent a great deal of thought, hours of shopping time, and every spare nickel she'd been able to scrape together on the perfect gown for her recital. At last she'd found it: plain, ankle-length, loose enough to flow gracefully when she walked out on stage and sat down at the piano, slim enough so that she wouldn't get lost in it. Lantern sleeves would hang down to flatter her too-thin arms when she made her entrance and took her bow, then fall back to leave her hands and wrists free as she played.

The color was the gown's greatest attraction: a rich, glowing scarlet that picked up the warm flush in her skin tones and made a dramatic background for the long, dark hair she'd had when she bought it. It could not have been called a pretty dress for a sweet young girl. Persis hadn't meant it to be. It was a practical, effective costume for a serious performing artist. And it was not in the garment bag.

As usual, Muriel Green had thought she knew best. What she'd sent was the gown she herself had chosen back in February, for her younger daughter to wear at the engagement party and the various other evening affairs Persis hadn't been able to get out of attending since then. It was supposed to make its farewell appearance tomorrow night, at a so-called family dinner the Greens were giving for the Cowleses.

As far as Persis was concerned, her mother couldn't have made a worse choice. The gown was the same insipid mauve shade as her maid-of-honor gown, in a slim-skirted Empire fashion with a belt up under her armpits and a wide neckline that left her knobby collarbones on full view while her arms were stuffed like sausages into glove-tight sleeves clear down to her knuckles.

Looking silly was bad enough. Wearing a dress that wouldn't let her take a full step or bend her elbows without a struggle was plain agony. Persis had managed to endure it at the parties, where all she'd had to do was stand around and be part of Loni's background. She hadn't been too bothered about having to put it on again tomorrow night because she expected to be miserable then, anyway. But tonight, how was she supposed to make her entrance and exit in a skirt that was too narrow for more than a mincing shuffle, or take her bows with that off-the-shoulder neckline falling away to show everything she had? Worst of all, how could she play the piano in sleeves that wouldn't permit freedom of movement in her wrists and elbows?

Persis must have looked as stricken as she felt. Miss Folliott, who normally wouldn't have noticed anything except a muffed G-sharp or an adagio that ought to have been an allegretto, said, "Good heavens, what's the matter?"

"My mother sent the wrong dress," Persis choked. "I can't play in this thing."

Miss Folliott took the hanger out of her hand, shook the mauve nightmare loose from the garment bag, and held it up to the light.

"Oh, dear, I do see what you mean. One of your sister's, I suppose? It certainly doesn't look like you. But we can't do anything about it now, Persis. You're on for the overture in about a minute and a half. You'll just have to grin and bear it, I'm afraid."

"In those tight sleeves?"

"No, the sleeves will have to go."

Calmly and ruthlessly, Miss Folliott took hold of the dress and ripped. Stitches popped. The sleeves came away, leaving raw edges and hanging threads around the armholes.

"There you are, my love. Put it on, quick. Here, duck behind this screen so people won't see you. Whatever possessed you to cut off all your beautiful hair today of all days? You might at least have fanned it out over your shoulders to cover the damage."

"Don't talk about it. That was my mother's idea, too," Persis snarled.

Miss Folliott said, "Oh dear," again, zipped Persis up the back, and went to comfort a third-grader who'd come down with a fit of the hiccups. Persis smoothed the skimpy skirt down over her narrow hips and tucked away the ragged edges as best she could. Her bare arms looked a mile long, her hands as big as Minnie Mouse's. One fleeting, agonizing glance into the mirror showed her head like a fuzzy peanut with those shaggy wisps sticking out in all the wrong places.

Miss Folliott gave her a once-over, snatched the blue chiffon stole from around her own shoulders and draped it over the mutilated bodice. "Here, wear this. And for goodness' sake try to keep it down over your arms as much as you can. It's not so bad, Persis. Really it isn't."

Chapter 2

It was a gallant lie, but it didn't make Persis feel any better. Going before an audience in that makeshift getup took nerve. Luckily she didn't have to play anything difficult at this time, just appropriate music to keep the early birds entertained while the late-arriving parents and grandmas and doting aunties were finding seats, dropping pocketbooks, and rustling programs.

"What's appropriate?" she'd asked Miss Folliott.

"Oh, some Strauss and perhaps a little Rachmaninoff or Schubert. Easy stuff. You know."

So Persis began a rather sentimental prelude she'd learned when she was about eleven. A tall, stoutish man in the second row looked up at her with a pained expression and closed his eyes.

He needn't think he was getting away with that. As it happened, Persis had played for the high school glee club a few months before, when they'd put on a College Night. During rehearsals, she'd learned a good many of the rousing old songs with which students had for ages been rattling the windows in the halls of academe. Keeping her eye on the sullen sleeper, she cut her prelude short and crashed into the opening bars of "Fill the steins for dear old Maine." His head jerked up, he caught her eye and began to grin. She grinned back and gave him the "Michigan Fight Song."

This was fun. She had the whole audience with her she could feel them responding. Okay, now it was safe to go on to Strauss. The "Blue Danube Waltz" wouldn't send her new buddy back to sleep, surely. She'd played that so often she didn't even have to think about the notes.

Not like playing her concerto. She still hadn't dared confess to Miss Folliott that she didn't have her music with her. Theoretically it didn't matter because the students were supposed to have their recital pieces memorized. In practice, though, it was all too easy to forget and have to be prompted in a hurry.

Even though she was feeling chilly in her now sleeveless dress, with nothing but Miss Folliott's flimsy blue scarf between her bare arms and an air conditioning vent that was blowing straight at her, Persis began to sweat. Forget it, she kept telling herself. You can worry about the concerto later. Concentrate on what you're playing now. Little did that man in the second row realize what a favor he was doing her by needing to be kept awake.

The two seats in front of him were still empty. These were the pair Persis had reserved for her own parents. They'd show after the intermission, most likely. During the nine years since she'd begun taking lessons with Miss Folliott, the Greens had attended enough recitals to know the littlest kids were always put on first, so that they wouldn't have to wait around getting sleepy and cranky before their turns came to play.

Persis herself was going to be the grand finale this year. By now, she was not only one of the oldest students, but far and away the best in the group. That wasn't bragging but simple fact. For one thing, most of Miss Folliott's pupils quit taking piano lessons when they got into their teens and their lives got cluttered up with too many other activities. Or else they went away to private schools—Donville was that kind of town—or their fathers got transferred by the corporations they worked for.

Persis's father would never be transferred because he worked for his father-in-law. He'd married the boss's daughter and was still hoping to become president of the firm himself some day. So far, Muriel Green's father had shown no sign of quitting, so Charles Green was still stuck with being Grandpa's assistant.

And Persis had stuck with her lessons. She truly loved the piano. Practice had never been a bore to her. Her marks at school were only average and she didn't always turn in her homework on time, but when it came to music, she'd been a model student. She'd shown up on the dot with her lessons prepared, she'd remembered everything Miss Folliott taught her and used her knowledge in the right places. She'd made up her mind when she was ten that she was going to be a professional musician and had consequently developed a grown-up approach to her playing that surprised some people and either amused or annoyed the rest.

Being so totally goal-oriented hadn't made for all-around popularity. Persis seldom had time to hang out with her friends; there was always practice, a rehearsal, a gig to play or a lesson to give, since she'd been taking some of Miss Folliott's beginners for the past year or so. Even the students she played with in the school orchestra got annoyed with her sometimes. Persis had this thing about wanting to quit horsing around at rehearsals and get down to making music.

Other people's opinions didn't worry Persis much. She didn't care to be everybody's pal, she wanted to be a good pianist. She'd already begun to make her mark, earning top awards ever since she'd been old enough to participate in local and regional music competitions. Only two weeks ago, she'd won the statewide gold medal. None of her family had been there to see her get her award because one of the neighbors had been giving a shower for Loni that night. Her mother had been angry with Persis for being hurt that her parents wouldn't be at the competition.

"For goodness' sake! I went last year, didn't I? And a more boring evening to sit through I never want to get stuck at again. I should think you might pass up the competition for once yourself. How often does your only sister get married?"

"That remains to be seen," Persis had replied. Her remark had not eased the tension. When she'd gotten home with her medal, she hadn't even bothered to tell her parents she'd won it. If they didn't care about her, why should she care about them?

She finished "The Blue Danube" and went on without thinking to Anton Rubenstein's "Melody in F." The man in the second row gave her a look of hurt reproach. She threw him an apologetic shrug and switched to the "Whiffenpoof Song." This would be her last selection. Miss Folliott was in the wings, signaling that they were ready to begin. She must be wondering where the Whiffenpoofs came from. Who cared? At least Persis now had one friend in the audience. She was almost sorry to leave him to the tiny tinklers and their nervous renderings of "Dolly's Funeral."

"Well, you were having fun out there," Miss Folliott remarked when she got offstage.

"There's a guy out there in the second row I was trying to keep from falling asleep," Persis explained. "The tall one in the gray suit. I'd have played him a few Sousa marches if I could have remembered any."

"It's a good thing you didn't." Miss Folliott's voice sounded a bit strange. She was either annoyed with Persis or having an attack of nerves. Most likely nerves, Persis thought gratefully, when the teacher added, "Tie Petey's shoelaces, will you? I don't want him falling on his face before he gets to the piano. No, Karen, you may not wear bright purple lipstick on stage. Your mother would kill me. Fix her face, Persis, and start lining them up in order of their appearance. Got a program? Here, take this one. Come on, Betsy, you're next."

Trying to cope with Miss Folliott's jitters, Persis

didn't have time to develop a case of her own. She didn't start to panic until she'd given a pat on the back to the last performer before her and stood alone in the wings listening to Miss Folliott tell the audience, "I'm sure my other students will forgive me for saying we've saved the best till the last because we're all so proud of our interscholastic champion. Here she is, this year's gold medal winner, Persis Green."

Everybody started to clap. Persis gave one last, frantic hitch to the blue chiffon stole and prayed she wouldn't stumble in that narrow skirt. As she went on-stage, she heard Miss Folliott's urgent whisper.

"Persis, your music!"

"Vladimir Ashkenazy doesn't carry music," she muttered out the side of her mouth, and kept on going. Right now, she couldn't call to mind a single note of her concerto. She could only hope her trusty hands remembered.

They did. After the first few tentative notes, she simply let go and let the music happen. By the time she finished, Miss Folliott's dainty scarf was a sweat-soaked rag around her neck, the raw seams at her armholes were sticking out, the hairdo Antoine had spent so much time fussing over was a worse mess than he'd left it, but even the man in the second row was on his feet yelling, "Bravo!"

All right, so she wasn't Vladimir Ashkenazy. Maybe her concerto had been nothing more than a welcome contrast to all the Fairy Dances and Teddy Bear Marches. Who cared? What musician was going to quarrel with a standing ovation? Persis took her bow regardless of what might be happening at her neckline, was called back for another, grabbed her teacher by the hand and dragged her back to share the third. Miss Folliott hugged her in front of everybody.

That was when Persis thought to look down at the two seats she'd so carefully saved in the front row. They were still empty. Like a true professional, she managed to get offstage before she started to cry.

Chapter 3

"Persis?" One of her own little pupils was tugging at her skirt. "Are you okay? What's the matter?"

"It's only a nervous reaction, Susie," Miss Folliott explained. "It's not unheard-of for a musician to cry after a performance."

"Sometimes it's the audience that cries." Persis blew her nose on a tissue Miss Folliott handed her and tried to laugh at her own woes. "I'm all right, Susie. I couldn't eat before I went on. Maybe I'm just hungry."

"We did have some punch and cookies."

Miss Folliott looked around the backstage area, but could find only empty paper cups and a plate with some crumbs on it. That figured. Persis had to be a good sport about missing the cookies, too.

At least now she could get out of this wretched straitjacket. She found her jeans and jersey and ducked into the ladies' room. By now, the dressing room was too crowded with parents looking for their budding geniuses. No Greens among them, of course.

Persis dragged out the business of changing her

clothes as long as she decently could, wondering how she was going to get home. Miss Folliott or somebody would give her a lift, she supposed, if she asked. Some joke, the star of the evening having to thumb a ride after the show.

She was hurt but not really surprised that her father hadn't shown up. He'd been finding more and more excuses to work late at the office, with the wedding so near and things at home so frantic. But her mother had promised. It was pretty stinking of her, after Persis had even sacrificed her hair for the sake of that awful gown they were foisting on her.

Maybe she'd been afraid Persis would make a scene, and she had reason to be. She'd known perfectly well Persis had intended to wear the red gown for the recital. She'd seen it when it came home from the dress shop and thrown a fit because Persis had gone ahead and bought it without consulting her first. Sending the mauve horror had been no mistake; she'd done it on purpose, and she was going to hear about it in no uncertain terms. Persis stuck out her tongue kiddishly at the cropped head in the ladies' room mirror, splashed cold water over her face to remove the tear streaks, and went to see what was happening backstage.

Nothing much, actually. Most of the crowd had cleared out. One or two parents were still wandering around hunting for various articles their childen had mislaid, or stopping to chat with other parents while their offspring hung around them whining, "Come on, let's go. You said we could stop at the Dairy Queen."

Miss Folliott was wearily picking things up and stuffing them into shopping bags. Some man who looked vaguely familiar was leaning against the edge of a table, fiddling with his car keys and watching her. He must be waiting for Miss Folliott to finish her chores so they could go. Her boyfriend, Persis assumed, if boyfriends could be old and fat. Fairly old, anyway. Well, probably not much older than Miss Folliott. Persis felt a little annoyed at the notion that her piano teacher could have a man interested in her.

Then she realized why he looked familiar. This was her friend from the second row. Apparently it hadn't been the teacher he was waiting for, but Persis herself. When he caught sight of her coming toward him with the mauve dress over her arm, he slid off the table and stood up straight.

"So there you are. Not a bad performance, Miss Green."

What did he mean, not bad? Persis scowled at him. "Maybe you could have done better?"

Miss Folliott gasped, "Persis!"

The man only jerked his head toward the stage entrance. "Come on."

Wishing she'd kept her big mouth shut, Persis followed him. He sat down, flipped his coattails over the piano bench and stretched his arms to loosen his sleeves. Even before he'd struck the opening chords of her concerto, she realized what an utter fool she'd made of herself. After a few bars, he glanced up at her with the same grin on his face she'd seen when she played him "The Stein Song."

"How'm I doing?"

"Mr. Lanscome, I'm sorry," she blurted.

Well she might be. The last time she'd seen Frederick Lanscome at a piano, he'd been on stage at Symphony Hall and she'd been up in the second balcony wondering if she'd ever get to be anywhere near half as good.

He let his hands fall. "Sure you wouldn't rather hold out for Vladimir Ashkenazy? Was that really why you wouldn't bring your music out with you?"

"No," Persis admitted. "It was because I didn't have any to bring. I left it home and forgot to tell my mother to send it with the dress. I didn't dare tell Miss Folliott for fear she'd pass out."

The famous pianist thought that was a riot. The next thing Persis knew, she was telling him the whole story about her horrible day. He nodded in perfect sympathy.

"You don't have to tell me, young woman. Wait till you go on tour. That's when old Lady Luck really socks it to you. I once had to appear on live television before a symphony audience wearing light blue slacks and tan shoes with an evening jacket I borrowed from the third trombone. The producer stuck me behind a low screen and threatened to break my jaw if I made the mistake of standing up to take my bow. I'll bet I was more nervous then than you were tonight."

"I'll bet you weren't," Persis said.

"But you came out here and laid 'em in the aisles all the same. That's what counts and don't you ever forget it. It is a shame about your red gown, but it's a far worse one about that gorgeous hair. Do me a favor and let it grow back before you come to us, will you?"

"What do you mean, come to us?"

"Hasn't Angela told you?"

Miss Folliott, who'd come onstage when he'd started to play, shook her head. "I haven't had time, Frederick. Persis, you of course know about the Master Classes for Piano Mr. Lanscome sponsors over in Lowrey. The thing is, he wants to offer you a scholarship."

"Me?" Persis gasped.

Frederick Lanscome nodded. "I was one of the judges at the statewide finals. You wouldn't remember because I had to dash off right after we'd finished judging and I don't think you ever saw me. Frankly, I was surprised to encounter a performer of your caliber in that age group. Which isn't to say you don't have a long way to go yet," he added, in case she might begin to feel too pleased with herself.

"When Angela told me you were one of her students, I thought I'd come along tonight and see how you shaped up in a repeat performance. I have to admit I needled you a little bit at the beginning there, on purpose, to see how you'd react. You came through like an old pro, which pleased me very much. That knack of reaching out to an audience is one thing that can't be taught. As for the concerto, you were a bit tentative the first couple of bars, but now that I know why, I guess I can't hold that against you. So how about it. Do you think you might be interested in studying with us for the next few years?"

Persis ran her tongue around her dry lips. "I'd be crazy to say no, wouldn't I? I mean—well, of course! What would you—" She couldn't finish the sentence.

"What's the deal? It's not a free ride, I can tell you that. What we offer is what we call a working scholarship. You'd have to provide your own living quarters because we don't have any dormitories, but you're close enough to commute so that's no problem. We do have a dining room where you'd get your meals without charge. Some of our students work there, but I think we could use you to better advantage as an assistant instructor in our junior classes. Angela tells me you've already had some teaching experience with her."

"Yes, and she's done very well," Miss Folliott put in. "The children really like her."

"Good. And you'd also accompany other musicians in both practice sessions and performance. If it's a school-sponsored program you don't get paid; but we do have a good many outside requests for accompanists, and you often can pick up a fee that way. In any case, it's professional experience you wouldn't be apt to get at most schools. The scholarship would also save your family a fairly hefty sum of money, if that's any consideration."

"It is to me," Persis answered. "They were planning to send me to the same dumb junior college my sister went to. I've been fighting tooth and nail to make them let me study music instead, but they won't listen. My grandfather says it's not practical."

"Here that, Angela?" said Lanscome. "You and I have been wasting our time being impractical all these years."

She laughed. "Too bad we didn't know sooner. Persis, I am sorry your parents weren't able to come tonight. It would be nice if we could settle this matter right here and now. Of course I know it's a busy time for them," she added out of politeness.

"What do you mean, busy?" Frederick Lanscome demanded. "What's more important than their daughter's recital?"

"My sister's wedding," Persis told him. "It's the biggest thing since *Star Wars*. There's no sense trying to get them to listen to anything about me till after June twenty-fourth. About the Master Classes, Mr. Lanscome, do I still have to finish high school before I can come? I was going into my senior year."

She hoped he'd say she could come right along, but he didn't.

"You finish. As far as this coming year goes, Angela seems to think she's taken you to the point where you'd be better off having your weekly lessons at the school. Think you could manage the commute? We can work out a time that will suit your schedule. And it's part of the scholarship."

"I can manage," Persis told him. "I'm old enough for a driver's license and I've already passed my driver ed, all but the road work. I might be able to talk my parents into letting me have my sister's car after she gets married."

That was pure wishful thinking. Loni wasn't the sort to let anything out of her grabby little mitts if she could help it, and Chet might not be inclined to buy her a new car right away. No matter, the bus service between Donville and Lowrey wasn't bad.

"Besides," she said, "my grandmother lives in Lowrey. I could stay with her if it stormed or anything. She has a foldaway bed."

"Good," said Frederick Lanscome. "Then it's just a matter of talking things over with your parents and getting the go-ahead. Now, Persis, since you don't have transportation tonight, may Angela and I offer you a ride home? I thought we might stop somewhere for a bite on the way. I don't know about you, but I'm always starving after a performance."

Chapter 4

"You're always starved before one, too."

Angela Folliott was laughing at the famous pianist, teasing him as if he were just anybody. She looked young and pretty all of a sudden, Persis noticed. Or was that because Persis was seeing her tonight in a different frame of reference?

After all, she'd known Miss Folliott all the years she'd been growing up. When she was seven, Persis supposed, anybody over ten would have looked old to her. Besides, she'd never thought of Miss Folliott as a person, particularly, but as a piano teacher. It was a revelation to find that she was not only a human being but a delightfully amusing companion.

The impromptu supper party was a great success. This was the first time in her life Persis had been out with two people much older than she who were ready to treat her not as a child but as another person like themselves, somebody they could talk with about things that interested them all equally.

Who'd have thought that after such a disastrous

29

day she'd wind up sharing a pepperoni and mushroom pizza with the great Frederick Lanscome? That she'd be chatting with him about Brahms in much the same way as her friends at school discussed their favorite rock stars—only, she told herself, far more intelligently. It was a wrench when her fabulous new acquaintance said at last, "Well, Angela, I expect we'd better get young Persis home to bed so she can let her hair grow."

"I should say so," her former teacher agreed. "I didn't realize how late it was getting. You must be done in, Persis. Maybe we ought to have called your mother. She'll be worrying about where you've got to."

"I doubt it. She's probably asleep by now."

But Persis was wrong. Though it was after midnight by the time Frederick Lanscome walked her to the door, both her parents were still sitting in front of the television set in the family room. She burst in on them, forgetting she'd been hurt by their indifference, wanting only to share her triumph."

"Guess what!"

Muriel Green shot up out of her chair and whirled around like a cornered tigress. "Never mind what. You just listen to me, Persis Green! If you ever humiliate me like that again—"

Persis couldn't believe what she was hearing. "Like what? Mama, they gave me a standing—"

"I don't know what you're talking about and I don't want to hear it. All I know is that you've made me a laughingstock in front of Marcia Powell and heaven knows who else. Ruining that lovely dress out of sheer spite! Wasting all that money—"

"How do you know about the dress?"

"Because I saw you in it, of course. And that's the thanks I got. I'd been running my legs off trying to get hold of that woman who's supposed to be getting the napkins and matchbooks printed up and being stalled off again till I'm almost frantic. And then I made a special effort to get over to the auditorium, even though I was ready to drop and it was so late I thought I'd probably find the recital over and done with. And what happens? I open the door to the auditorium and there you are, strolling out on the stage in front of that whole audience with your bare arms hanging down to your knees and some piece of blue rag wound around you like an old woman going to market. I was so humiliated, I just shut the door, turned around, and came straight on home. Eighty-nine dollars and ninety-five cents I paid for that dress, and you rip it to shreds as if it were—well, don't just sit there like a bump on a log, Charles. Say something. She's your daughter."

Charles obliged. "And that was my ninety bucks, in case you didn't happen to notice. What's the big idea, Persis? You think I'm made of money?"

"You think I wanted that stupid dress in the first place? Mama bought it, I didn't. And she's the one who sent it to the auditorium after she'd made me late getting this ghastly haircut I didn't want, either. That's another thirty bucks down the drain, but you needn't start yelling at me for spending it."

Mrs. Green started to say something, but Persis

wasn't finished yet. "Mama, you knew perfectly well I meant to wear the red gown I bought with my own money. I picked it out because it was a dress I could play in, which the one you sent me wasn't. It isn't ruined, we just had to take the sleeves out because you can't play the piano if you can't bend your arms. You never thought of that, did you? And if you were embarrassed, how do you think I felt?"

Persis stormed up to her room, still clutching the plastic garment bag with the mauve dress inside, even though she hated the sight of it, too hurt and furious even to cry this time.

She didn't sleep very well, which wasn't surprising. At about half-past six she gave up the struggle, remembered it was Saturday, got out of bed, and noticed that loathsome bundle slung over the chair where she'd dumped it. Now what was she going to do? If she didn't get the miserable thing repaired somehow so she could wear it tonight when the Cowleses came to dinner, she'd never hear the last of it.

Persis thought a minute, then rolled up the garment bag, which also held the torn-out sleeves Angela Folliott had insisted she bring back with her, and tied a belt around it for easier carrying. She took a quick shower, dressed a little more carefully than she normally would have on a morning when she didn't have school, sneaked down to the kitchen with the rolled-up garment bag in her hand, got herself a glass of milk and a doughnut, and slipped out the back door.

It was a two-mile walk to the bus station, but Persis

didn't mind. The exercise was a good way to work off tension. She caught the eight o'clock bus with plenty of time to spare and was halfway to Lowrey when it occurred to her she might have been smarter to phone ahead and say she was coming.

Luck was with her, though. When she reached the somewhat rundown apartment house in an unfashionable part of the city, she found Gran Green still in bathrobe and slippers, coming to the door with a cooking spoon in her hand.

"Persis! This is a surprise."

"I know, I should have telephoned first. Sorry, Gran."

"Forget it, dearie, I'm glad to see you. How did you get here? Is your father downstairs?"

"No, he doesn't even know I'm here. I came on the bus."

"All by yourself?"

"Gran, I'm a big girl now. If you want the truth, I'm in a jam with the folks. I was hoping you could bail me out."

Persis unrolled the garment bag and pulled out the mangled remains of her ninety-dollar mistake.

"So that's how it happened, Gran," she said after she'd told the dismal tale of how the dress had arrived there in three pieces. "Mama's spitting tacks about the dress, and Daddy's mad about the ninety dollars. And they're giving that ridiculous dinner for the in-laws at the house tonight, and I was supposed to wear this thing again. I thought you might possibly be able to sew the sleeves back in or something, so they wouldn't keep jumping down my throat about it."

Her grandmother took the mauve dress from her, looked at the torn armholes, checked the sleeves. "Oh, I expect we can cobble it back together somehow. I just don't see why you want to wear the silly thing anyway. I didn't care for it on you at the engagement party, and I don't suppose it's going to suit you any better after we get it fixed."

"I didn't say I wanted to wear it, Gran. Mama says I have to because it harmonizes with Loni's, as if anybody was going to notice. And I'll never hear the last of that ninety dollars if I don't. Honest, I'll be so glad when this damned wedding's over!"

"Persis, what have I told you about swearing?"

"That it's a sure sign of an ignorant person who can't think of a more intelligent way to express herself," Persis mimicked. "Look, can't I do some shopping or something for you while you fix the dress?"

"You can walk over to the stores with me in a little while, if you want to, and help carry the bundles. This shouldn't take too long. They can't have sewn the sleeves in right in the first place, or your Miss What's-her-name couldn't have ripped them out so easily. Ninety dollars for a shoddy rag like this!"

Charles Green's mother always made a point of not criticizing her daughter-in-law openly, but she was pretty capable of letting a person know what she was thinking. "But quit dithering on the doorstep, child. Come into the kitchen. I don't know what possessed me to make blueberry pancakes this morning. I haven't had them in a coon's age."

"You must have heard me coming." Persis was beginning to feel better. "It's just as well you've kept in practice. You're going to be seeing a lot more of me before long."

Chapter 5

"How's that, dearie?"

At last Persis had a willing audience. Her grandmother listened to every word about the gold medal and what it had led to, asking all sorts of questions, to most of which Persis didn't yet have answers.

"A full scholarship! And to think he made that special trip last night to hear you. He must think you're pretty good, dearie. And you'll be having lessons here next winter, too? What happens if you run into bad weather?"

"I'm glad you asked. Would it be okay if I brought my sleeping bag and parked it behind the garbage pail or somewhere, in case I get stuck for a place to sleep?"

"You don't need to bring a sleeping bag. There's that perfectly comfortable sofa bed in the living room, and I'm not so hard up I can't spare you a couple of blankets. I wonder if that medal's really gold?"

"Probably not. Gold's awfully expensive these days. Dad was yelling about it the other day. Loni wanted to give her bridesmaids gold charms, but they'd have cost far too much. She'd picked out the most adorable little piano for me," Persis added rather wistfully.

Gran Green sniffed. "What would you need a thing like that for? You've got your medal, haven't you? Solid gold or painted tin, you won it fair and square. First in the whole state, imagine! Wait'll I tell them down at the bingo parlor. Come on, dearie, finish up that last pancake. You don't have to worry about your figure. Maybe you'd like to clear away the dishes for me while I take a look at your dress."

"Sure." Persis mopped up the syrup on her plate with the last wedge of pancake, then got up to deal with the sticky plates.

She liked this apartment. She'd been parked with Gran every so often when she was younger and her parents had some engagement in Lowrey, and she had always enjoyed those times. After she'd gotten old enough to be left at home with Loni or by herself, which amounted to the same thing for practical purposes, she hadn't been here much.

Somehow, the family never seemed to get around to visiting Gran except on Mother's Day or her birthday or some other special occasion when they could come bustling in with an armload of presents to show how much they cared. Muriel Green would do most of the talking while Gran served tea and the rest of them sat around wondering how soon they could leave.

For certain functions, Charles Green would drive over and get his mother and take her back to Donville. She'd been at Loni's engagement reception, for instance, in a new gray polyester dress she'd made herself. Persis had thought how nice and grandmotherly she looked. Loni had fussed afterward about getting Gran fixed up for the wedding so she wouldn't look so dowdy compared to the rest of the older women. Chet's grandmother was having her gown custom-made.

"Gran's is custom-made, too," Persis had argued. "That only means having something made specially for you and nobody else, in case you're too dumb to know."

Naturally, that had led to another big blow-up. Her father had asked her when she was going to get smart and learn to keep her mouth shut. Persis had thought that was pretty crummy of him, since it was his own mother she'd been sticking up for. She sometimes wondered if her father was ashamed of Gran because she was no more than decently provided for instead of filthy rich like his in-laws.

Gran was far better company than her mother's parents, anyway. They pushed the shopping cart around, cracking silly jokes over the groceries, then went on to the hardware store, where Mrs. Green bought some vacuum cleaner bags and told the manager all about her granddaughter the genius.

She didn't mention the scholarship because Persis didn't have anything in writing from Frederick Lanscome yet and Gran was a firm believer in not counting chickens before they hatched. A medal, now, that was different. You could set it up on the mantelpiece to show your friends when they dropped in for a cup of tea after the weekly bash at the bingo parlor. Persis must be sure to bring it with her when she came next time, so the neighbors wouldn't think Mrs. Green was making up fairy tales in her old age.

"You're not old," Persis protested loyally.

"Yes I am, dearie. I'm a precious antique, like this stuff in Trotter's window. My stars, will you look at the prices? Why people want to fork out good money for stuff somebody else was glad to get rid of—well, I do declare!"

Gran Green paused in front of the antique shop and peered through the glass. "If I'm not mistaken, that's a twin to my great-grandmother's cake basket, the one I gave Loni for a wedding present. And that she hasn't got around to thanking me for, I might add. I wonder what Trotter's asking for it. Can you see the tag?"

"No, it's stuck down into a crease in the cloth." The antique dealer had his wares tastefully set out on a swirl of faded blue velvet. "Want me to go in and ask?"

As it happened, she didn't have to. Mr. Trotter, who must have been having a dull morning, came out to see what they were so excited about.

"Something I can help you with, ladies?"

"We were just wondering what you're asking for that silver cake basket," Mrs. Green told him. "That one back there with the knob broken off the handle."

"Knob broken off?" Mr. Trotter was affronted. "Oh, no, madam, that piece is perfect in every way. A superb example of late Federal silver craftsmanship."

"That's as may be," said Mrs. Green, "but if you take a good, hard look at the handle, you'll see where there used to be a little ivory knob in the shape of a pineapple, right at the top. I know because I've always had to be so careful of mine when I polished it."

"An ivory pineapple, eh?" That interested him. "And you say you actually own a duplicate? Could I ask where you got it?"

"It came from my mother's family," she told him. "My mother always claimed her own mother had had a pair of them. She could remember her sister and herself each having to pass one around when the minister and his wife came to tea. I've often wondered where the other one got to."

"Interesting," murmured the dealer. He'd picked up the graceful serving piece and was going over it inch by inch with the aid of a little magnifying glass he'd stuck up to his eye.

"Yes, I do see now where there could have been a tiny mounting broken off. The handle's been repaired so expertly nobody would ever notice. But those carved ivory pineapples were certainly characteristic of the period. The pineapple is a symbol of hospitality, as you perhaps know, and it was often used in ornamentation. And you say yours still has the ivory knob?"

"It did the last I saw of it." Mrs. Green was enjoying herself, Persis could see.

"You wouldn't by any chance be interested in selling? If it's something you never use any more—"

He slitted his eyes and gazed at her shabby coat. Gran Green had never been particularly clothes-conscious, and she didn't see why a person had to get all rigged out like a hog going to war, just to impress the cashier at the supermarket.

"I might go as high as two hundred dollars," he coaxed.

"And you might go a darn sight higher when you wrote up the price tag," she retorted. "What's that one marked at?"

"Well, naturally we have to take a legitimate profit. How else could we stay in business? Two-fifty?"

"Aren't you going to show me the price tag?"

"Five hundred, and that's my final offer."

"Which means you'd resell it for at least a thousand. I'll think about it. Come along, Persis. We still have that dress to finish."

As they went on down the street, they heard a wild shriek of "Five-fifty" wafted on the breeze toward them. Gran chuckled.

"If Loni doesn't want that cake basket, tell her to send it back to me. I shouldn't be surprised but what we might beat Mr. Trotter up to six hundred, if we took the notion."

Chapter 6

The dress came out better than Persis could have hoped. Instead of replacing those straitjacket sleeves, Mrs. Green had ripped them apart and used the material to make puffy little caps that would be more comfortable on a warm night. She'd bought rich lilac ribbon downtown and used it to perk up the insipid mauve bodice with pipings and a belt with long streamers that hung down over the skirt. It still wasn't Persis's style, but at least it wasn't blah.

As a crowning touch, she presented her granddaughter with an engraved gold locket on a handsome gold chain. "Here, dearie, this was my great-grandmother's, too. I'd intended to give it to you for a graduation present next year, but you might as well have it now."

"Oh, Gran, that's beautiful! You shouldn't."

"Why shouldn't I? If everybody else is hanging gold medals on you, I guess I can, too. Now you'd better scoot along or you'll miss your bus. And carry the dress carefully so you won't get it wrinkled and have to press it again when you get home. Here, hang the garment bag over your arm, like this. And spread it out over the seat when you get on the bus, if you're lucky enough to get one. I'll see you at the wedding."

"Aren't you coming to the rehearsal dinner?"

"It's all part of the same thing, isn't it? Near enough as makes no never mind, anyway. Watch out for that hem, you're letting it drag. Sure you don't want a sandwich to take with you and eat on the way?"

"Oh, sorry." Persis snatched the open end of the bag up off the floor. "No, I'm still full of pancakes. They were great. Thanks for everything."

A quick kiss and she was off again, feeling infinitely better than when she'd come. The bus wasn't crowded, so she was able to share a seat with the mended gown. She even managed to catch one of the scarce local taxis when she got back to Donville, which saved her having to walk the two miles home. When she got there, she found her mother in a tizzy, as she'd anticipated.

"Persis, where have you been, will you tell me that? I've called all over town trying to find you. You've got to go down to the bridal shop this instant. They said they'd try to find something for you to wear tonight, since you so kindly demolished that lovely mauve gown I paid—"

"It's all fixed," Persis interrupted. "See?"

She held up the garment bag. For once, Muriel Green couldn't find anything ready to say. Persis's father, coming downstairs unshaven and blear-eyed from sleeping the whole morning away, had plenty.

"What's this, for God's sake? Another ninety bucks?"

"Nope, just the price of a bus ticket to Gran's. I told you the dress wasn't ruined. Gran fixed it, better than new."

Persis took the dress out of the garmet bag and held it up for her parents to see.

"Hey, not bad. Not bad at all. Try it on, Puss."

Charles Green must be really pleased. Puss was her baby name. He hadn't called her that in ages. Muriel Green wasn't giving up without a struggle, though. She didn't care much for those cap sleeves because they'd show Persis's bony elbows too much. She didn't see why her mother-in-law had spoiled the effect with all those gaudy ribbons. But she supposed it would have to do, since Persis's father was in one of his stingy moods. And it was nice of Gran to give Persis that gold locket, though she wondered why the elder Mrs. Green hadn't seen fit to send the bride something. After all, this was Loni's wedding.

"Do you have to remind us?" Persis growled. "She did send something, in case you've forgotten. How about that late Federal sterling silver cake basket she brought over last time she was here and hasn't even got thanked for yet? If Loni doesn't like it, Gran says she'll be glad to take it back. We saw one just like it only with the little ivory pineapple on the handle broken off in an antique shop this morning. Gran told the guy she'd inherited a mate to the one he had, but with the pineapple

44

still on, and he almost went out of his skull."

"What?" snapped her mother. "Persis, are you making this up?"

"Go see for yourself. It's in a window over in Lowrey. That place near the hardware store. First he offered Gran two hundred, then he went up to five, but he wouldn't show her the price on the one he was selling, so she knew five hundred was peanuts compared to what he expected to get, and turned him down. Then he practically chased us down the street yelling, 'Five fifty.' So I told her Loni was crazy about the basket and the note must have got lost in the mail or something."

Muriel Green turned in bewilderment to her husband. "Charles, do you honestly think—"

"Mother was putting him on? Why should she be? I suppose you thought that cake basket was some old piece of junk she'd had kicking around the house. My folks weren't exactly beggars, you know. At one time, they were a darn sight better off than—"

"All right, Charles, I've heard that one before. I never said anything against your family, did I? And antique silver has appreciated tremendously in value these past few years. What did he call it, Persis?"

"Late Federal. That means after the Revolution. Early eighteen-hundreds, I suppose. The pineapple was a symbol of hospitality and widely used at the time in ornamentation," she quoted as nearly as she could remember.

"Late Federal. Hospitality." Muriel Green gave herself reminders as she ran to get the cake basket from her husband's den, which she'd preempted for housing the wedding presents.

"This really is an exquisite thing," she gloated, coming back with the gleaming silver serving dish in her hand. "Look how beautifully that little pineapple's carved. And of course it makes the piece more valuable. I must get over to Lowrey first thing Monday morning and find out what he's asking for the mate."

"You're not planning to buy another one?" yelped Charles Green.

"No, Charles. I'd like to know, that's all. A fine old family heirloom! You know, Charles, that was awfully sweet of your mother. Nancy Cowles will be sick with envy. This is one thing she could never buy, with all her money. The Cowleses haven't an ancestor among them. Not one they'd care to admit to, anyway. Not that it's anything against them," she added hastily. "Loni'd better phone her grandmother right away instead of waiting to write a note. She's so touchy, she might take a notion not to come to the wedding. She did say she's coming, didn't she, Persis?"

"Oh yeah, she's planning on it. I'm not sure about the rehearsal dinner."

"Oh, but she can't miss that! Not after giving us such a valuable gift. She's got to back me up about the cake basket, tell how it came into the family and how long they'd had it, that sort of thing. Otherwise Nancy will think I simply went out and bought it. Take your dress upstairs and hang it in your closet before you tear it again. I hope you thanked her properly. And get Loni up. She'd better talk to her grandmother right away so she won't be late for her manicure appointment. I don't know why everything always winds up falling on my shoulders."

"I don't know why a man can't get a bite to eat in his own house," was Charles Green's complaint. "That damned maid won't even let me in the kitchen."

"Mary's sore because Mama's making her work tonight," Persis told him. "Her boyfriend was going to take her roller skating. I'll get you something."

Persis and Mary got along fairly well, as a rule. A little coaxing and she was back in a few minutes with coffee, some leftover potato salad and cold cuts, and a couple of buttered rolls on a tray. "Okay, Dad?"

"That the best you could do?" he grunted.

"Yes."

"All right. You needn't snap my head off like everybody else around here. How's Mother?"

"Fine. She made blueberry pancakes."

Her father looked at the tasteless bakery roll, sighed, shrugged, and stuffed half of it in his mouth. "What else did you do?"

"Nothing special. We went grocery shopping. And she fixed the dress and I washed the dishes."

"How come she gave you the locket?"

"She thought it might take my mind off that lousy dress. Besides . . ." Now was the time. Persis hadn't felt any too happy this morning when her grandmother

47

had said, "Charles must be tickled to pieces about your winning the gold medal and the scholarship," and she'd had to reply, "I haven't told him yet."

"Say, Dad—"

She didn't get to finish. Her mother's voice came through the door, loud and shrill. "Hold on a second, Mother Green. Loni wants to—Loni? Persis! Persis, where's Loni? What are you standing around down here for?"

"I was getting Dad some lunch."

"Couldn't he have waited two seconds? I told you to wake Loni. Your grandmother's on the phone. Well, move, can't you? Tell Loni to get on the upstairs extension, quick. And don't forget to remind her about the cake basket."

Just for the sake of argument, why couldn't her mother have waited another two seconds to put in the phone call, if it came to that? Persis had sense enough not to ask. She grabbed the mauve dress, ran upstairs with it, roused her unwilling sister from a nest of ruffled eyelet pillows with little blue bows on them, and propelled her to the telephone.

"It's Gran Green. You've got to thank her for the cake basket."

Loni yawned. "That old thing?"

"It's a valuable antique."

Loni woke up. "How valuable?"

"At least a thousand dollars. Probably more."

"Really?" Loni picked up the phone, all sweetness and light. "Hello, Granny darling."

48

Persis left her sister cooing into the mouthpiece and went to hang up her remodeled gown. So now Dad would get on the phone with Gran and hear the news from his mother instead of his daughter. So what?

As she left her bedroom, however, she met him coming upstairs to shave and dress. "Dad, aren't you going to talk with Gran?" she asked in surprise.

"I said hello downstairs before Loni got on."

"Was that all you said, just hello?"

"If there's anything else to say, your mother's already said it."

He went into his own room. He probably didn't mean to slam the door in Persis's face, but that was what happened.

That slam set the tone for the rest of the day. Persis didn't even get time to practice. Her mother screamed if she or anybody else even went near the living room, where the baby grand stood in the bay window at the far end, for fear an ashtray might get pushed half an inch out of place or a footprint be left on the freshly vacuumed carpet.

Charles Green gave up the struggle and went to play golf at the club. Loni trotted off to her manicure. That left Persis to do the odd jobs for her mother and the increasingly disgruntled Mary, who'd already given notice twice that week and mustn't be allowed to quit until after the wedding. She didn't dare balk at helping, because she could sense that her mother was already about two screaming fits away from a nervous breakdown. Somebody had to stay sane, whether she liked it or not.

ᒐᐧᑭᐧᑭ Chapter 7 ᑭᐧᑭᐧᑲ

The dinner party was about what Persis had expected. To begin with, Grandma and Grandpa Dane showed up half an hour before anybody was ready, carrying presents and expecting a royal welcome.

"Here you are, Muriel dear," said Grandma Dane. "I brought some yummy petits fours, and a dozen lovely, fresh eclairs. Now you won't have to bother about dessert."

"But, Mama, I have dessert already arranged," Muriel Green protested weakly.

"Then just pop yours in the freezer and save it for another time, darling. What's happening in the kitchen? I'll run out and make myself useful while you dress."

"No, please!" Mary was on the verge of quitting again, as it was. "Everything's under control, Mama, honestly. What I'd really love is for you to—"

Persis caught the little pause. What Mama would really love was for Grandma to go away and come back when she was supposed to. What she said was, "—to come upstairs and help me and the girls finish dressing."

"Women!" snorted Grandpa Cowles. "Why couldn't you be ready on time, Muriel, for once in your life? Take these, Charles. I figured I'd better stop and buy you a box of decent cigars. Cowles turns up his nose at anything but Imperials."

Persis wished her father would reply, "I know. I got some yesterday." But he only smiled in a sickly sort of way and muttered, "Nice of you to think of them."

Then Grandpa helped himself to one of the cigars, sent Charles to fix him a drink, and settled himself in the best easy chair, scattering newspapers and cigar ashes around the living room his daughter had been so desperate to keep clean. Persis decided she might as well go upstairs and finish getting changed.

When she got to her room, she found Grandma Dane rummaging through her dressing table.

"Oh, there you are, Pussy dear. Where on earth do you keep your hair spray?"

"I don't have any," Persis told her. "It's bad for the environment."

"But, sweetie, how do you ever expect to catch a husband if you don't learn the importance of good grooming? Now you sit right down on this stool and let Grandma fix your hair. Loni always had the loveliest hair, right from the day she was born. Those sweet little blonde curls and that dear little innocent baby smile."

"Yeah," said Persis. "She hasn't changed a bit."

"Now, darling, I know we can't all be like Loni, but we can make the most of what we have. I always say it's not what you look like but what you are underneath that counts."

And so on and so on and so on, until it was time to go down and listen to the women talk about the upcoming wedding and the men about their golf games; and watch Loni and Chet go through their lovebird routine with about as much animation as Persis's old Barbie and Ken dolls. What they thought about this charade, if they thought at all, Persis could not imagine.

Since nobody was paying her any attention, Persis had nothing to do but sit back and watch. It was curious how Mama turned into a second Loni when her own mother was around. She and Daddy were acting exactly like Loni and Chet, being good little kids in front of their elders.

So were Chet's parents. That pair were about as exciting as two bowls of tapioca pudding, Persis decided. At least her own parents knew how to keep a conversation going. Once her father even remembered to throw a remark her way.

"Enjoying you new dress, Puss?"

That was supposed to be a joke, but Grandma Dane took it as a personal compliment, for some reason.

"Muriel and I picked it out together. Muriel has lovely taste. Gets it from my side of the family, they say. People always tell us we're more like sisters than mother and daughter. Don't they, Murrie?"

"Yes, Mama," Mrs. Green answered obediently. "Could I give you a tiny bit more of the Pommes Duchesse?"

"No, sweetie. I'm saving room for an eclair."

One more round to Grandma Dane. Persis wondered when they'd get to eat the Baked Alaska that was supposed to have been the grand finale of the meal. Never, most likely. Why couldn't grandparents mind their own business?

She supposed she ought to be thankful Chet's folks had brought only one set of ancestors with them. His mother's relatives weren't coming up from Florida until the day of the rehearsal dinner. Tonight there were just the elder Cowleses to endure. They were more than enough. Chet's grandfather kept interrupting everybody to remind them he was even richer than Murton Dane, therefore even more entitled to their undivided admiration. His wife was, if possible, worse. She had Grandma Dane's trick of picking you apart and showering you with compliments in a pitying way that made you feel not only like an idiot, but like a homely idiot with rotten taste and no manners.

As far as taste went, Persis thought she'd never seen anything more revolting than the bright blue satin dress Mrs. Cowles was wearing, unless it was the enormous brooch she'd pinned to her shiny bosom. The brooch was in the shape of a heart with a red ribbon wiggling down across its middle. Persis entertained herself with picturing how the brooch would look attached to the back of her bicycle as a reflector while Mrs. Bowles was letting her hostess know the sparkling stones with which the heart was solidly paved were real diamonds. The red stones that made up the ribbon were genuine rubies, and not baby ones, either. Mrs. Cowles told her presumably enraptured audience the exact number of diamonds and rubies involved, and how much they added up to in carats.

"It's insured for ten thousand dollars, Muriel. I want you and Charles to know that. Because"—she unpinned the brooch from her bosom with a fine, dramatic flourish "—this is going to be my personal wedding present to Loni and Chet."

Everybody was properly flabbergasted, especially the bride-to-be. Surely Loni must realize what a great, vulgar hunk of ostentation she was getting stuck with. She might not have brains, but she did know good from ghastly when it came to personal adornment. Nevertheless, she rose to the occasion, fluttering and exclaiming and running around the table to kiss her future grandma-in-law, pretending she thought Old Man Cowles was cute when he pinched her on the panty girdle.

"Let me pin it on for you," he kept insisting.

Loni wasn't that dumb. "I can't," she told him. "Chet bought me this beautiful orchid corsage, and I wouldn't dare do anything to spoil the effect. You'd hate me forever, wouldn't you, sweetie-pie?"

Sweetie-pie obediently said he would. Anyway, there wouldn't have been room for all those carats, with so much expensive purple foliage sprouting over the tiny bodice of her frock. Loni's was mauve like Persis's, also cut in the Empire style. The design and color were perfect for her slighter build and delicate complexion. Even Persis had to admit she looked enchanting as she leaned over the embroidered tablecloth and lifted the floral centerpiece off the mirrored tray on which it had been sitting.

"I'm going to put the brooch right here in the middle of the table where everybody can get a good look," she said. "There, isn't that gorgeous?"

Persis thought the mirrored tray made the brooch look twice as large and even more hideous, but she dutifully agreed with the rest that it was gorgeous. Then Mary served the champagne, forgetting to wrap a napkin around the bottle until Muriel Green hissed at her. They all drank to generous grandparents who gave wonderful presents. When the champagne ran out, Mrs. Green moved her party into the living room, carrying the brooch before her on the tray as if it were the crown jewels at a coronation.

While her elders sipped their coffee and liqueurs, Persis sat trying not to yawn, wondering how a roomful of people could manage to be such a pack of bores without seeming to realize how dull they were. Escape was hopeless. If she moved or spoke, somebody took it as a signal to send her for a drink of water or some clean ashtrays. She didn't mind the going so much. It was the coming back that was tough.

Muriel Green had set the trayful of rubies and diamonds on the piano. That led Chet's mother to ask, "Who plays?"

Persis said, "I do," hoping she'd be asked to perform so she could impress them with her concerto, or at least "The Whiffenpoof Song." But old Mrs. Cowles launched into a monologue about how she'd hated piano lessons when she was a girl, so her daughter-in-law had to say she'd hated them, too. Then her son said he'd never understood what anybody could see in that highbrow stuff, and the grandfather took up the tale of how he'd once got dragged to a classical concert and gone into a make-believe coughing fit so he'd have an excuse to get up and leave. They were all supposed to think that was funny. Persis was going to tell him it wasn't, but her mother caught her eye and gave her a look.

She settled back into sullen silence. Might as well sulk if she felt like it, nobody was paying attention to her anyway. Even if she were to bring out her gold medal to show them, they'd only say it wasn't worth insuring and how could she waste her time on that highbrow nonsense anyway?

Persis thought they'd never go; but at last they did, in a great bustling and babbling, planning to meet tomorrow for Sunday brunch at the country club. Loni didn't try to hide her relief as her allegedly adored Chet went off with his family. Nor did she greet him with delight when he rushed back.

"What's the matter?"

"My grandfather left his gold pencil."

Mrs. Green started into the living room after Chet, but he was already running out again.

"I found it. Got to go. They're waiting."

Loni yawned, not at all prettily. "Thank God that's over. I'm going to bed."

"You might help your mother straighten up first," said Charles Green, hoping thereby to get out of doing it himself.

Loni was already halfway to the landing. "Why can't Mary?"

"She took off for the roller-skating rink as soon as dinner was over," said Mrs. Green wearily.

"Then let Persis help you. She's got nothing better to do. I'll be a wreck tomorrow if I don't get some sleep."

Loni yawned her way out of sight. Charles Green grabbed the depleted tray of liqueurs and took them back to the dining room. His wife flapped around, walloping sofa cushions into place, moaning about a scratch on the coffee table, then scooped up as many glasses and coffee cups as she could carry.

"Bring the rest, Persis," she said, and headed for the kitchen.

That left Persis alone in the living room. Automatically, she wandered over to the piano. There, next to a pile of music, lay that ten-thousand-dollar bicycle reflector, winking up at her from the mirrored tray. She picked it up, just to see how it felt to hold so much money in her hand at one time. Then she reached down behind the sofa and pinned the brooch to the upholstery.

She could never have said why she did it. Maybe she was still resenting the fuss they'd all made over the brooch while ignoring her. Anyway, there it was, hidden from sight, and here came her mother shrilling,

"Persis, what's keeping you? Haven't you got that stuff picked up yet?"

"I'm coming."

She ran around snatching china and crystal off the end tables, then sprinted for the kitchen. Much of the fragile tableware had to be washed by hand, and her parents unanimously elected her to dishpan duty. That was all right with Persis. She could pretend she was back in the apartment with Gran Green. Sloshing around in hot soapsuds was far less disagreeable than listening to Grandpa Dane and Old Man Cowles trying to out-pontificate each other.

She was sleepy after the heavy meal, the late evening, and her early-morning journey. So she'd almost forgotten her impulsive prank with Mrs. Cowles's monstrous gift, until she heard her mother shriek from the living room.

"Charles, the brooch! It's gone."

"Oh, for crying out loud! Calm down, Muriel. Loni took it upstairs with her, naturally. Where else would it be?"

"She did not take it upstairs."

"Then why the hell didn't she? If she hasn't got sense enough to take care of a ten-thousand-dollar hunk of jewelry, she doesn't deserve to have it."

"She'd have left it for me to put away. Loni's not ready for that kind of responsibility."

"So what's she getting married for?"

"Charles, do you have to pick me up on everything I say? You haven't even deigned to mention how well

58

the dinner went off, after the way I slaved to get ready."

"Okay, the dinner was great. What's that got to do with the brooch? Persis, go ask your sister what she did with it."

"I'll go myself. Try and get anybody to do anything right around here."

Muriel Green went off sputtering. Her husband shrugged.

"I wouldn't put it past old Cowles to have palmed the thing himself on the way out. Maybe he's trying to make it look as if we were careless and let the brooch get stolen, so he can collect his ten grand from the insurance company."

"But, Daddy, how could he?" Persis protested. "His wife already gave the brooch to Loni."

"Not on your life she didn't. She gave it to Chet and Loni as a wedding present. There's a nice little legal distinction there. What it means is that she meant the pin to stay right in the Cowles family, and don't try to kid yourself it won't."

"That's a relief." Persis turned on the faucet spray to rinse a handful of forks. "I'd hate to think I ran any risk of ever having to inherit that monstrosity myself. Did you ever see anything uglier in all your life?"

"What are you talking about? Real diamonds and rubies."

"Daddy, it's just an expensive piece of junk. Loni will never wear it. Unless she happens to take a course in belly dancing. It might look okay hanging over her bellybutton."

"Nice talk for a young girl, I don't think. Oh, Christ, now what?"

Muriel Green was screaming again. "Charles! Charles, Loni says she didn't take it."

"Huh? Where is she?"

"She'll be down in a second. She's getting her robe and slippers on. She says it was still on the piano when she went to bed."

"How does she know?" Persis objected. "She went out in the hall to wave bye-bye as soon as the Cowleses started to leave, and she never went back into the living room after that for fear she'd get stuck with picking up a few dishes."

"That's right," said Charles Green. "Remember, Muriel? I told her to help you straighten up, but she said let Persis do it and went upstairs."

"Then I suppose she meant it was still there when she last looked. What difference does it make? Don't just stand there. Come and help me hunt for it."

Persis hung back a little, making a production of drying her hands. She'd let them sweat for a couple of minutes, then go in and find the brooch behind the sofa. Not too quickly or they'd smell a rat. She'd better put on a little show of poking around under chair cushions and stuff first.

When she went into the living room, Loni was at the piano, shuffling carelessly through Persis's music and complaining about the fuss. "It slid off the tray and got stuck here somewhere among the pages, most likely. I don't know what you're acting so hysterical about,

Mama. It's not your diamond and ruby brooch, you know."

"That's not your music you're ripping to pieces, either," Persis reminded her. "Let me do that. I know more about pianos than you do."

"Oh, Persis, you're impossible!" snapped her mother.

Mrs. Green shoved both daughters aside and began scrabbling through the piles of music herself. That was fine with Persis. She drifted off to the other side of the room and began picking up seat cushions.

"What are you wasting time over there for?" shrilled her mother. "How could the brooch have got clear across the room?"

"Somebody might have taken it to look at and dropped it down among the pillows," Persis argued—convincingly, she hoped. "They were all half sloshed by the time they left."

"They were not!" Loni protested.

Charles Green overruled her objection. "If they weren't they ought to have been. The way old Cowles swilled down my best brandy, you'd have thought he was drinking Pepsi-Cola. Which chair was he sitting in?"

That was the cue Persis had been waiting for. "On the sofa," she said. "I'll look."

She did her performance with the seat cushions, then ran her hand down over the back. All she could feel was nubbly tweed upholstery.

The ten-thousand-dollar brooch was gone.

Chapter 8

That was when the nightmare really began. Persis shoved the sofa away from the wall and scanned every inch of it by the strongest light she could put on, although she could not see how she could ever miss that blazing headlight if it had been where she'd put it. She searched the carpet. She even lay down and squinted along the pile, in case the brooch might have fallen and landed face down so that the stones weren't reflecting the light. Nothing.

Between them, she and her mother practically tore the living room apart. Loni stood weeping into the sash of her baby-blue negligee. Charles Green trotted around after his wife and daughter, picking things up and setting them straight, bleating, "Save the pieces, can't you?"

They kept at it for hours. After they'd searched the living room right down to the wallpaper, they carried the hunt to the front hall, the coat closet, the downstairs powder room, the dining room. They even searched the stairway and Loni's bedroom in case she might have carried the trinket upstairs with her and forgotten she had it, which was absurd but showed the state they were in by that stage. Again they found nothing.

At last they called a halt and fell into bed, so exhausted that all four of them slept late and almost missed getting to the country club in time to keep the appointment with Loni's future in-laws.

"Now remember," Muriel Green whispered to her daughters as they were going in, "don't say a word about the brooch unless they do, but be extra nice to show how appreciative you are. If anybody asks why Loni isn't wearing it, you say it's not appropriate for a bride to wear such lavish jewelry until after she's married. If they ask what we did with the brooch, tell them Daddy put it away for safekeeping. Got that?"

"For the eighty-second time, yes." Loni sighed. "Fix your hair, Mama. It's all over your face."

Muriel Green did a fast repair job, then stuffed her comb and mirror back in her purse. "Now smile, everybody. Come on."

"What a gruesome charade," Persis muttered as she pasted a kind of snarling grin to her mouth and followed the rest of them into the club lounge. Loni performed like a professional, though, rushing up to Chet's parents with happy little cries, being girlish with Grandma and Grandpop, paying no attention whatever to Chet. If that was love, Persis would take pistachio.

Charles Green was exuding the kind of bogus geniality that might have been expected from a salesman trying to sell a used car. Persis had the impression that everybody else was doing the same. Finally she got tired of grinning and nodding and faded into the background. She wasn't missed. Nobody paid any further attention to her, until Todd Ormsey drifted over.

"Hi, Persis. What's up?"

She ought to feel flattered, she supposed. Todd only noticed the pretty ones, as a rule. He'd been one of Loni's boyfriends until Chet Cowles's family had been checked out as being more fiscally solvent than the Ormseys, and Chet himself easier to nudge altarward. Todd was too foxy for Muriel Green to manipulate.

"Hi, Todd," she replied cautiously. "We're having brunch with the Cowleses."

"So I gathered. You've done something to your hair."

"Don't remind me."

Persis could see herself reflected in one of the mirrors that hung around the walls of the lounge. Her mother had been too flustered by their late rising to tell her what to wear, so Persis had put on her favorite deep pink shirt with a softly gathered gray skirt, pink strappy sandals, and her grandmother's handsome gold locket. She'd also dunked Antoine's revolting hairdo under the shower and given it a quick fluffing with her blow-dryer for a more natural effect. She still didn't like it, but at least the reflection in the mirror didn't make her sick.

Persis noticed another face in the mirror. Muriel Green was looking at her and Todd with a strange expression; but then Chet's mother said something and Muriel had to put her smile back on, quick.

"No, honestly, I think it's great," Todd was insisting. "Makes you look more grown up."

Persis didn't quite know what to say to that, so she changed the subject. "Still got your Fiat?"

"No, I got rid of the Fiat a few weeks ago. It was giving me problems. I'm driving a real classic now, a white 1967 Sting Ray."

"How come?"

"Had a chance to make a deal, and grabbed it."

Todd went into a lot of technical detail about why he'd been so smart to take the Sting Ray. None of what he said made any sense to Persis, but she listened anyway, wondering why Todd Ormsey was squandering so much of his famous charm on Loni's kid sister all of a sudden. Then she realized he wasn't. He was using her to put on an act for Loni's benefit, making her see what she'd passed up for Chet Cowles.

Furthermore, Loni was getting the message. Persis wasn't surprised when their twosome was ever so neatly turned into a foursome, and she herself got maneuvered into making small talk with Chet while Todd took Loni over to one of the big picture windows to feast her eyes on the white Sting Ray.

That didn't last long. Muriel Green called sharply, "Loni, tell Chet we're going into the dining room now." Loni bade Todd a laughing farewell and came over to take Chet's arm.

"Time's up, Persis. Chet belongs to me now. You're

just the maid of honor, remember?"

How could she forget? Persis faded back again and got snared by her mother.

"What was Todd Ormsey handing you a line about?"

"It wasn't a line," Persis replied sulkily. "He was only telling me about his new car."

"What new car?"

"A 1967 Sting Ray."

"Huh. Down to driving old clunkers, is he? I'm not surprised, considering the shape his father's in with the SEC. Did he ask you to go for a ride in it?"

"Fat chance."

"Well, if he ever does, don't you dare say yes. You hear me? Todd Ormsey's no fit companion for a girl your age."

"He was fit enough for Loni, till Chet turned up. Besides, a 1967 Sting Ray isn't a clunker, it's a classic."

"I don't care what it is. You stay out of it."

Muriel Green rearranged her upper lip into more agreeable contours and went back to telling Grandpa Cowles how wonderful he was, as if he needed to be told, while they walked in and joined the line for the brunch buffet.

The meal was endless. Persis got so sick and tired of so much talk about nothing that she kept going back to the buffet and getting more food she didn't want, merely for the sake of something to do. Then dear, kind Grandma Cowles pranced up to the dessert table and got her a huge, gooey pastry to top it off. So she stuffed down the dessert out of politeness and had to sit through a lecture from her mother about getting too fat to fit into her maid of honor gown.

Even getting away, at last, from the Cowleses didn't improve the situation. Muriel Green went into another anxiety attack about the missing brooch. Charles Green was sleepy and cross because he'd eaten too much and had had to miss his usual Sunday morning game of golf. Loni was in one of her moods, silent one minute, flighty the next, finally throwing a temper tantrum and storming upstairs.

When she came down, she was wearing tight designer jeans, cowgirl boots, and a brown suede jacket and cap that belonged to Persis. That was a surprise. Loni seldom liked any of her sister's clothes well enough to borrow them.

The suede jacket was special, however, soft and beautifully tailored, though a bit heavy for an afternoon in early June. The cap had been bought big to acommodate the heavy head of hair Persis had still owned when she'd picked it out. On Loni's cropped head, the cap was so loose that it came down over her eyes, or would have if she hadn't propped it up with enormous sunglasses.

Persis felt a surge of fury, not only that Loni had taken her favorite clothes without asking but also that she was managing to look so much smarter in them than Persis did. She was about to raise a howl of protest, then decided she needn't bother. Her mother was already advancing to the attack.

"Loni, where are you going?"

"Out."

"What do you mean, out? Is Chet taking you somewhere?"

"Chet's tied up with his aunt and uncle. You heard him say so."

"I naturally assumed you'd be included."

"Well, I naturally assumed I wouldn't. I've had enough of that bunch for today, thank you."

"What are you going to do when you're married to them?" Persis couldn't keep herself from asking.

"I'm not marrying the whole family, dummy."

"That's what you think."

"Will you two quit bickering?" shrieked their mother. "Come and help me search the living room again. Maybe in the daylight—"

"Will you please shut up about that brooch?" Loni shrilled back. "I don't want to hear it. I told you I'm going out."

Muriel Green asked again, "Where?" but Loni's only answer was to slam the front door. Watching her out the window, Persis was surprised to see that she didn't get into her car, which she'd left parked out in front of the house since yesterday. Instead, Loni walked on down the street and turned the corner.

She was worried about her figure, no doubt, and had decided she'd better try to walk off some of that too-hearty brunch. Typical of Loni to do it in pointy-toed boots instead of comfortable walking shoes. She'd be limping and moaning before she got halfway around the block. Who cared? Persis had her own worries. How could that brooch possibly have disappeared from the back of the sofa?

It was senseless to search any more, considering how thoroughly they'd done the job last night. Nevertheless, Persis willingly joined her mother in the hunt, poking into nooks and crannies with a yardstick, fishing around inside the piano, feeling over every inch of the soft-piled carpet. At last she had to face what she'd been pushing to the back of her mind ever since last night. The brooch wasn't just lost. It had been stolen.

Then who took it?

Her mother had gone upstairs at last to lie down with an ice bag to her aching forehead. Her father was crouched in front of the television screen in the family room with a box of pretzels and a highball, watching a sports program. Rather, he was pretending to watch. He didn't even appear to notice when the action changed from a baseball game to a motorcycle race. All he wanted, Persis thought, was an excuse not to think.

That was how she herself felt. She'd have liked to play the piano, to drown her anxiety about the brooch in music. But how could she? The moment she touched the keys, her mother would begin screaming down the stairway about her headache, and her father would yell over the roar of the motorcycles, "Why the hell can't a man have a little peace and quiet in his own home?" She might as well go eat something.

Alone in the kitchen with a glass of milk and a

sandwich cut from last night's roast beef, Persis sat on a stool at the counter, racking her brain over who had taken the brooch, and how.

The how was easy enough. Unpinning the brooch from the sofa wouldn't have taken a second. She hadn't bothered to fasten the safety clasp when she'd committed her insane prank of stabbing the pin into the upholstery. She couldn't recall whether she'd left the pin pointing up or down. If that heavy mass of frozen assets had been in a position where it could swivel around, she supposed it would have been dragged out of the cloth by its own weight. If it had fallen on the plushy wall-to-wall carpeting, though, it wouldn't have made enough noise to be heard and investigated. And fishing it out would have involved either pulling the sofa away from the wall or getting down on the floor and pawing around behind. That would have taken time and almost certainly have attracted notice from some other member of the family. So it had more likely been taken from the spot where she'd put it.

Yes, but how would the person who took it know it was there? Maybe that wouldn't have been so hard, either. The living room was roughly thirty feet in length, but not more than eighteen feet wide. The sofa had been the logical place to hide the brooch, if there was any logic connected with this crazy situation, simply because it happened to stand at the far end of the room near the piano. It sat parallel to the wall, but not tight against it because the baseboard heating ran behind.

Persis had simply leaned over the sofa and pushed the pin into the back, at the end that was closer to the piano. Therefore, it probably hadn't really been all that well hidden, and it was in the area that had been searched first. Quite possibly one of the others—Loni, her father, or her mother—had gotten the entirely reasonable idea that the pin had been accidentally knocked off the piano and kicked behind the sofa. They'd have turned on the strong reading lamp that stood on the table beside it, seen the stones glitter in the light, and instead of shouting, "Here it is," or whatever, have scooped up the brooch and kept it. The one place they hadn't searched last night was in each other's pockets.

Because Muriel Green was always the one who did things around the house, Persis's thoughts turned immediately to her mother. But that was ridiculous. Look at the way Mama had spent hours and hours searching, insisting that the others help her. She'd still be at it, no doubt, if her head weren't aching so badly.

On the other hand, Mrs. Green's head had been aching all day. She'd complained of a headache as soon as she'd gotten up and taken two aspirin before they'd set out for the club. She'd said afterward they hadn't done a bit of good, yet for three or four hours she'd smiled and chatted and played the perfect hostess to Chet and his family. Anybody would have thought she hadn't a care in the world beyond making sure her guests had a good time.

Nor was this by any means the first time Persis had watched her mother putting on a performance. Muriel

71

Green could out-act any soap opera heroine when she chose to do so.

That didn't mean she'd stolen her own daughter's wedding gift. Why should she? Mama would never be able to wear the brooch, surely. Even if she had the stones reset in a different design, everybody would know where she'd gotten them. Besides, resetting all those little rubies and diamonds would be an expensive proposition in itself.

Of course, she could sell some of the jewels to pay for the work. Maybe that had been her idea: to sell not some of the jewels, but the entire brooch. Mrs. Green had been spending tremendous sums of money on this wedding. She and her husband had already had some awful fights over the bills. Were there still more and larger bills, that she hadn't even dared show him?

There were places where you could get jewelry copied. Persis had overheard some of her mother's bridge club buddies talking about having it done. You parked your genuine forty-carat diamond necklace in the family vault and wore the rhinestone copy, and nobody was supposed to be able to tell the difference.

Persis had wondered at the time why, in that case, a person didn't simply settle for the copy and sell the original to buy something really worth having, like a Steinway concert grand. Apparently, though, you had to keep the real one stashed away or it didn't count.

Everybody in their crowd must have heard by now that Chet's grandmother had presented him and his fiancée with her own heart-shaped diamond and ruby brooch insured for ten thousand dollars. If they hadn't, they would, soon enough. That meant Loni would have to appear in public wearing the brooch after she was married, but it could also mean she'd get away with wearing a copy instead of the genuine article.

Right now, the brooch was of no practical use to the Greens. Loni wasn't supposed to wear it yet, nor could it be left out on display unless Charles Green hired a detective to guard it. People would assume they'd put it in a safety deposit box at the bank, most likely.

Persis thought about all those wedding gifts her mother had been exchanging ever since the invitations went out. Loni had begged to keep some of them, but that hadn't cut any ice with Muriel Green. What did Loni know about keeping house? What did anybody know about anything, except Mama herself? Why should she hesitate to do what she pleased with this latest wedding present?

The only hitch was, Mrs. Cowles's gift wasn't like any of the others. Mrs. Green wouldn't dare take it back to the jeweler for a simple refund, even if she knew where it came from. There'd be the question of the insurance, to begin with. Even Mama must have sense enough to know she'd never get Daddy to go along with a scheme that amounted to something pretty much like grand larceny. She could hardly expect Loni and Chet to let themselves be robbed without a squawk. So why couldn't she have hit on a scheme to trick her family into thinking the brooch was lost, at the one time when it could most easily be spared, and then to stage a big recovery scene when she'd had a duplicate made to be found in place of the original?

Muriel Green would do a lot to get her own way. Look at how she'd practically sabotaged Persis's recital by sending the wrong outfit when it was too late to correct the mistake. Look at the way she'd stormed out of the auditorium in a rage when she'd seen how the gown had had to be mutilated so Persis could perform in it.

Persis didn't honestly believe her mother had acted out of spite. She had simply taken it for granted that her own choice had to be better than her daughter's. She'd probably convinced herself she was doing Persis a favor. If she took it into her head that Loni's interest would be best served by stealing the brooch and selling it—would she really go that far? Persis hated to think so.

Still, she'd done some pretty weird things under the mounting stress of the past few months. Was she actually beginning to crack up?

In any event, if the brooch suddenly reappeared in a week or so, and if the diamonds wouldn't scratch glass the way her science teacher back in sixth grade had demonstrated with her own engagement ring, the truth would be clear. As to what she'd do with the information, assuming she ever got it, Persis hadn't the faintest idea.

Chapter 9

She finished the milk, brushed up the sandwich crumbs with a paper towel so she wouldn't get screamed at for leaving a mess in the kitchen, stuck the empty glass in the dishwasher, and went back to the family room.

Her father had fallen asleep in his chair with the television still blasting. A bowling tournament was in progress now. The crash of the pins didn't seem to bother him. Persis thought again of getting in a little time at the piano, but that would mean shutting off the set and no doubt he'd jump up frothing at the mouth if she did.

Anyway, playing the piano involved going into the living room, and she'd spent enough time there already. She got a sick feeling at the pit of her stomach every time she caught sight of the sofa.

No matter which of the others had taken away the brooch, it was her fault for having moved it off the piano in the first place. If she'd left it lying there in plain sight, probably nobody would have thought to carry her lousy practical joke one step further. She drifted miserably back to her own room, flopped on the bed with a book, and tried to read. Instead, she fell asleep.

After such a wild weekend, Persis had reason to be exhausted. She would no doubt have slept heavily until Monday morning, clothes and all, if the telephone hadn't waked her.

After a few tries, she managed to get her eyes open. It was pitch dark in the room. Who could be calling at this hour? Anyway, the call must be for Loni; it usually was. The two sisters had a private telephone line they were supposed to share, but Loni'd always gotten the big end of the deal. Why wasn't she answering the phone? Surely she must have got home from wherever she'd gone by this hour, especially since she hadn't taken her car.

Home or not, she wasn't going to answer. Nor was the caller going to quit, from the sound of that jangle. Grumbling, Persis got up and felt her way over to the dressing table, where her own white extension phone sat among her collection of miniature pianos and the plastic busts of Beethoven, Brahms, and Mozart. The digital clock beside it said twenty minutes to one. She picked up the receiver expecting to hear some drunk with a wrong number. Instead, she heard Loni.

"What took you so long?" Loni's voice sounded slurred and odd. "Persis, you've got to help me."

"Why? What's the matter?"

"Never mind. Look, I'm at a phone booth out on Cemetery Road. It's right beside the main cemetery entrance. You know, where there's a big iron gate and a couple of stone pillars."

"Yes, I know," Persis told her impatiently. "What are you doing there?"

"Quit asking questions, can't you? I've got to get home before Mama finds out or she'll kill me. For God's sake don't wake her up. You'll find a spare set of keys to my car in the top left hand drawer of my dressing table. Get them and drive out here, quick."

"But I can't take a car out on the road by myself. I've only got a learner's permit."

"Then don't get stopped. And hurry up!"

Before Persis could protest again, Loni hung up. What was the matter with her? Had she lost her mind? What sort of mess had she got herself into?

Even while Persis was thinking up fresh reasons why she'd be insane to take a car out on the road at this hour with only a learner's permit, she was in Loni's room rummaging for the keys. She didn't dare make a noise or turn on a light for fear her mother would think Loni was at home and come along the hall for a late-night chat.

Luckily, her sister was neat about her personal belongings. Persis found the keys by their feel and stuck them in the pocket of her jeans. That was another break, her having fallen asleep in the clothes she'd changed into after they'd come back from the club. She went back through the connecting door to her own room, grabbed a sweater, picked up her little purse, which still had a few dollars in it, sneaked down the back stairs, and let herself out the door.

Her third piece of luck lay in the fact that Loni's car was parked on the street instead of up in the driveway where it belonged. Persis had driven the foreign compact car once in a while before, when Loni had a burst of sisterly affection or a fresh manicure she didn't want to risk. In fact, Persis had been hoping to get in some practice driving with her sister to help qualify for her driver's license, but the wedding had put a stop to that.

At least she knew how to get the car started, but she didn't switch on the motor, not yet. Instead, she pushed the gear into neutral, released the hand brake, and let the car roll, without lights, down the hill as far as the intersection. She knew it was dangerous and no doubt illegal, but how else was she to avoid the chance of waking her parents? Now she had to hope some nosy neighbor wouldn't stir and think some kid was stealing Loni Green's car.

Once she dared start the car and switch on the lights, it wasn't quite so terrifying. Since she was still in a residential zone, Persis started off at a sedate twenty miles an hour. She was nervous about steering and too ready to jump on the brakes at the first sign of a deserted crossroad or a flickering shadow that might be a cat in the street but never was. Loni must be wondering what was taking her so long.

Well, okay. Persis was still wondering why Loni had yelled for help from Cemetery Road. Whatever could she be doing in such a place at this time of night? It wasn't like Loni to get into jams. She'd always been far too careful of her own swanlike neck for that.

Too soon she came to the highway. This was scary. The traffic signals weren't turned on at this hour; only the flashing yellow caution light at the intersection. How would she know when to turn? What if another driver came bombing along and didn't see her in time? Everything looked so different in the dark. Which lane was she supposed to be in? Persis held her breath, flashed her directional signal, and went.

She couldn't keep creeping along at twenty, not out here. If a police car happened along, they'd think she had engine trouble or something and stop her to find out what was the matter. She put her foot down on the gas pedal and gritted her teeth in panic as the small car leaped forward.

"Take it easy," she had to keep telling herself. "You're doing okay. Hang in there and don't blow it."

After a while, she began to get the feel of the wheel. This wasn't so terrifying. One or two cars passed her, going a lot faster than she dared to, but that didn't matter. They weren't paying any attention to her. She wasn't bothering them, over here in the right-hand lane, giving them plenty of room to get by. Let them go. It was fun in a way, having the road to herself.

But it was lonely, too. The further away from home she got, the stranger and creepier it felt. Persis reached the turn for Cemetery Road, flipped her signal again, and took it.

Now she was really alone. People stayed away from Cemetery Road, not because they were afraid of ghosts but because unpleasant things happened around here. Whatever had possessed Loni, coming to such a place by herself. How had she gotten here? Not walking in those cowboy boots, surely? The cemetery was close to ten miles from their house. Could she possibly have been hanging around the tombstones all evening? Persis didn't believe that for one second. She'd been somewhere, with somebody.

And Persis knew who it was. She remembered all too well, Loni, in a picture-book sheer mauve dress with big puffed sleeves and a bunch of artificial violets tucked into the sash, standing by that picture window back at the club with Todd Ormsey beside her, pointing to that white Sting Ray down in the parking lot. There'd been a wistful expression on Loni's face that Persis had never seen before. Maybe this was the first time Loni had faced the truth, that she was really going to marry Chet Cowles, that her days for racing around with handsome guys in sporty cars were at an end.

Loni wasn't the type to let go of anything easily. She must have fixed it up with Todd, right there in front of her mother and father and all those Cowleses, to meet somewhere for one last date before she and Chet tied the knot. That was why she'd left the house on foot, wearing her sister's clothes. Todd had picked her up somewhere nearby, and they'd gone off together. Then something had gone wrong.

And Persis could guess what. Todd had made the mistake of thinking he was going to get something for nothing. He'd forgotten Loni was a taker, not a giver. She'd made a deal with the highest bidder, and she wasn't about to risk spoiling her bargain.

The houses thinned out, the gravestones began to appear. Still it seemed a long, long time before the little car's headlights picked up the fancy wrought iron gates slung between the high granite pillars.

There was the phone booth Loni had called from, but where was Loni? Did she expect Persis to turn into the cemetery? Didn't she realize the gates were padlocked for the night?

Persis pulled up to the closed gates and braked but didn't shut off the engine. What if she couldn't get started again? What if some crazy guy came along? Did she dare give Loni a toot on the horn? Were those back windows shut tight? Was the door locked?

She'd worked herself into a full-scale panic by the time a slim figure darted out from behind the pillar that was closer to the phone booth, began fumbling at the door handle, pounding on the glass.

"Persis, let me in! What took you so long? Open the door, quick!"

"Just a second."

Sure now that it was Loni, Persis leaned over and released the catch. As the door opened and the dome light went on, she got a clear look at her sister.

"My God, what hit you?" she gasped.

Loni's face was smudged with tears and dirt, her makeup a mess, her hair in a mad tangle. Persis noticed a button gone from her suede jacket, and a hole in the leather where it had been ripped out. The front was revoltingly stained, reeking of liquor and vomit.

"What happened?" Persis insisted.

"Turn around and get going," was Loni's sullen answer. "Hurry up."

She wouldn't say any more, but huddled inside the ruined jacket, keeping her head down as if she were afraid of being seen. Persis didn't press her further just now. Whatever she'd done, this was no place to linger.

Darting frightened glances right and left, Persis managed to make an illegal U-turn and get the car headed toward home. Loni still wasn't saying anything. After a mile or so, Persis couldn't stand the silence any longer.

"Want to stop for coffee, Lon?"

"How can we? What if somebody sees us?"

"So what if they do?" Persis replied, to keep the dialogue going.

"Don't be stupid," Loni snapped.

"Look who's telling who. What happened to Todd?"

"What are you talking about?"

Loni's voice was so shrill and frightened, Persis knew she'd guessed right.

"Don't try to kid me, sister dear. You fixed up a date with Todd this morning at the club. You were going for a ride in the Sting Ray, right? Why else would you have left the house on foot the way you did? You never walk across the room if you can help it. So okay, did he make a pass at you or what?"

"Stop the car, quick!"

At first Persis thought Loni had some mad notion of leaping out. Then she glanced over at her and slammed on the brakes.

"You okay?"

Loni shook her head, shoved the door open, leaned out, and began to retch. At last she stopped making those horrible noises but stayed half in and half out of the car, huddled into a ball, shuddering. Persis reached over and hauled her back against the seat.

"Want a tissue?"

Loni nodded abjectly. Persis plucked a wad of the soft paper sheets from a box on the shelf under the dashboard and wiped her sister's face as best she could.

"Take it easy, Loni. We'll be home pretty soon. If the gas holds out."

Chapter 10

The gauge read dangerously close to empty. Kids at school were always making jokes about riding around on the fumes. Persis hoped that was actually possible; Loni was in no condition to walk. All she could do was keep nursing the car along, stealing a quick glance at her bedraggled passenger whenever she dared. Loni was a shade less green around the gills now that she'd gotten the liquor out of her stomach, but she was still awfully quiet.

"You'd better comb your hair and fix your face," Persis told her at last. "What if somebody's up when we get home?"

Loni started to cry again. "Don't say that!" she sobbed. "I'll die if Mama finds out."

"What's to find out? What happened to Todd? He tried to get funny and you wouldn't come across, so he ditched you. Right?"

Loni shook her head.

"You might as well tell me so we can get our stories straight, just in case. Where were you drinking?"

"A place Todd knows of," Loni admitted grudgingly.

"Where is it?"

"I don't know. Down toward South Springs."

"South Springs is at least sixty miles from here." Which wouldn't mean much to Todd Ormsey. He'd been picked up for speeding in far slower cars than a Sting Ray. "What sort of place was it?"

"Not the sort Chet's folks would go to, if that's what's worrying you."

"A dump, huh?"

Persis wasn't surprised. Todd had the reputation of never spending much on his women. Apparently he'd never felt he had to.

"Didn't you eat anything? What did you drink?"

"We had pizza and beer. Ugh!"

Loni clapped the handful of crumpled tissues to her mouth again, but she had nothing left to be sick with.

"Don't try to kid me," said Persis. "You didn't get like that on a couple of beers."

"Todd had a bottle of vodka in the car," Loni confessed. "Quit nagging at me, will you? You're worse than Mama. Can't I do what I like for once in my life?"

"When haven't you?"

"Never!" Loni exploded furiously. "Never once since I was born, if you want to know. Ever since I can remember, it's been, 'Loni, fix your hair.' 'Loni, don't muss your pretty dress.' 'Loni, smile for Uncle Peter.' Loni do this, Loni do that. If she ever said to me, 'Loni, forget how you look and have a good time,' I'd drop dead from the shock. Honest, sometimes I get so jealous of you, I could tear your eyes out."

"Jealous of me?" Persis couldn't believe what she was hearing.

"Why shouldn't I be?" Loni raged. "You go where you want, do what you like, and Mama never says a word. I break a fingernail, and it's a national catastrophe. So now she's got me wrapped up in Cowles Coatings, and I hope to God she's satisfied."

"Aren't you, Lon?"

"What have I got to say about it? Learn the facts of life, kid. Chet Cowles is a good catch, so Mama caught him. I'm just the worm on the hook. Worms don't talk, they squirm. Can't you go any faster?"

"No. I'm not taking any chances on getting stopped. Me without a license and you in that shape, they'd arrest us both."

Persis concentrated a while longer on not getting arrested. Then she asked, "Don't you love Chet?"

Loni shrugged. "Chet's okay."

"Is that all?"

Loni shrugged again.

"But you're going to marry him!"

"What am I supposed to do, wait for a knight in shining armor to carry me off on his nice white horsie?"

"A nice white horsie might be a darn sight safer than a white Sting Ray," Persis reminded her. "You still haven't told me what happened with you and Todd. Where is he now?"

"How am I supposed to know?"

"Where did you leave him?"

"Back there."

"In the cemetery? How come? What were you doing up there in the first place?"

"Talking. Having a drink. You know."

"I can imagine. So then what?"

"So then it got late, and I asked him to take me home. So he didn't want to. So I insisted. So Todd got sore and gunned his motor. So the car flipped."

"What? Loni, you don't mean you were in a wreck?"

"Not me. I wasn't in the car."

"What are you talking about? Can't you tell it straight?"

"Give me a chance. All right, if you want to know, I wasn't feeling very well. I knew I was going to be sick, so I opened the car door. Maybe he thought I was taking off, I don't know. Anyway, he switched on the ignition and I jumped out. I don't think Todd really knew what he was doing. He was pretty drunk."

"So he was alone when he flipped. Was he badly hurt?"

"How should I know?"

"But you were there. You knew he wrecked the car. Didn't you go to see?"

"Are you kidding? I beat it away from there as fast as my legs would carry me."

"But what if he was killed? Don't you even care?"

"Sure I care, but what could I do about it?"

"You could have gone to look. What if the car

caught fire? You might at least have gotten him out."

"Persis, will you stop it? There was nothing I could do, I tell you. I was so sick myself I could hardly stand up. The car made a lot of noise when it turned over. Somebody was bound to hear. I had to get out of there before anyone came, didn't I? If the Cowleses ever found out I was with Todd, they'd call off the wedding."

"Why should you care? You just said you're not in love with Chet."

"What's love got to do with getting married? Use your head, for God's sake. Everything's planned: the caterers hired, the gowns all bought, the invitations out. What about those presents Mama's been exchanging? We'd never get them straightened out. And they'd be after us to give back the brooch, and then where'd we be? Mama would skin me alive if I fouled up on her now. You don't know what she's like."

"That's what you think."

"Then quit talking like an idiot. Where are we? I can't see a thing."

"That's because you've got my cap down over your eyes. You sure picked a great time to borrow my best clothes. We're just coming to the playground, so we're almost home. Only I think we ought to go back."

"What do you mean, go back? We can't do that! I've got to get home. What if Mama wakes up and comes looking for me?"

"What if nobody heard that crash? What if Todd's still trapped in the car, bleeding to death from a slashed artery?"

"Persis Green, you take me home," Loni screamed. "I didn't make him wreck the damn car. Why should I let him wreck my life?"

"Then I'm going to phone the police right now and report the accident. There's a phone booth out behind the playground."

She'd called from that booth often enough herself in years past, asking her mother to pick her up after tennis or a volleyball game. She turned into the narrow drive that ran along the high chain link fence. Loni tried to grab the steering wheel and force her back on the road, but she was no match for Persis.

"Cut it out, Lon, or you'll wreck us, too. And quit screaming at me or I'll bend a few of your teeth out of shape. If Todd Ormsey dies, you'll be to blame for not reporting the crash. And so will I for letting you get away with it."

"But he'll say I was there."

"What if he does? You can lie out of it. You always do."

Persis found some change in her purse, slammed the car door shut on her half-hysterical sister, walked over to the booth, and dialed O.

"Could you please get me the Donville police station?" she asked the operator in the most la-di-dah voice she could manage. "This is an emergency."

She was half relieved, half terrified when she heard the ringing cut off and a deep voice saying, "Donville police. Sergeant Manley speaking."

"Hello." Her voice was shaking, but that didn't

matter. She'd sound more convincing. "This is Mrs.—" she made a noise that could have been anything. "My husband and I were over at the cemetery—"

"Doing what?" the sergeant asked in obvious surprise.

"Bird watching," Persis improvised. "The—the baby owls are hatching."

"Boy, that's a new one," she heard him remark to somebody at the station. "Got an owl-watcher on the line. Yes, Mrs.—ah, what did you say your name was?"

"Oh please listen to me," Persis whimpered. "We heard this awful crash. I was terrified! So we thought we'd better report it."

"You didn't try to find out what made the noise?"

"No. My husband wanted to, but I wouldn't let him. I was afraid it might be vandals wrecking the place. We came straight on home and called you. It was down on the far side of the hill, I think, away from the main gate. It could have been a car crashing into a tombstone," she added to salve her conscience. "People do drive up there sometimes."

"Okay, we'll check it out, Mrs.—"

"Thank you so much."

Persis hung up before he could ask again what her name was. She'd told him enough lies already. At least she'd done what she could. She got into the car and put the ignition key back in the lock. She hadn't dared trust Loni not to drive off without her.

Loni was still crying, but quietly now. Persis fished out some more tissues for her.

"Here, blow your nose. They said they'd send somebody."

"You didn't tell them who you were?" Loni snuffled.

"No, I made believe I was some woman who'd been owl-watching with her husband."

Loni actually managed to giggle. "How did you ever think of that?"

"I don't know, I just did. Don't you ever put gas in this heap?"

"There's enough."

There was, exactly. The motor died as Persis turned into their own street. That was all right; she'd entered at the high end of the hill after making that detour around the playground. All she had to do was switch off the lights and let the car coast to where it had been sitting before she'd driven it away, put it in "park" and pull up the emergency brake.

"Feels as if I'd been gone a million years," she said with a sigh. "Okay, Lon, you're home."

"You go in first," Loni whispered, "in case Mama's awake. While she's yelling at you for being out so late, I can sneak up the back stairs."

"You're a real sweetheart, you know that? Mama's not going to hear us. She took one of those pills the doctor gave her for her nerves."

"How do you know?"

Persis didn't, of course, but she figured she'd already stuck her neck out far enough for Loni.

"She always does. You know she can't get to sleep

without them, she's so keyed up over this wedding garbage. And if she can't sleep, she keeps Daddy awake, so you'd better believe he didn't let her forget."

"But Daddy might be up."

"Forget it. Daddy had a few drinks himself while you were lapping it up with Todd. He's out like a light. Take off those dumb cowboy boots and watch your step."

Somehow, Persis managed to strongarm her sister upstairs without waking either of their parents. Loni was in a state of total collapse by the time she hit the frilly white pillows, so it was Persis who got her undressed, cleaned up, and put to bed properly.

And it was Persis who sneaked back downstairs for a Coke from the refrigerator to quiet Loni's churning stomach, Persis who got rid of the panty hose Loni had ruined in her headlong flight through the ruined cemetery, Persis who sponged off the designer jeans and the beloved suede jacket Loni had been sick all over.

Persis felt pretty sick about that jacket herself. She'd never be able to wear it again, unless Gran Green had another trick up her sleeve. Why couldn't she have been an only child?

Chapter 11

It was a good thing Persis had taken that long nap Sunday evening. As it was, she informed her reflection in the bathroom mirror on Monday morning, "You look like an accident going somewhere to happen."

A long shower helped a little. She raked a comb through her wet hair, not bothering to hate the new haircut because she didn't have time, flung on a red and blue cotton plaid blouse and a denim wraparound skirt that reversed to the same plaid. It was a practical outfit to put on in a hurry because it didn't matter if you got the skirt wrong side out. Red canvas espadrilles and bare legs were accessories enough for a June morning.

Knowing the folly of skipping breakfast and then complaining all morning about being starved, Persis stopped in at the kitchen. She fixed a bowl of sliced bananas and cereal, poured milk, found a Danish pastry Mary had no doubt been planning to eat with her mid-morning coffee, and bolted it all at a rate that would have made her pediatrician faint dead away in horror. Satisfied, she leaped on her bike, pedaled like mad, and made it to her first class just as the bell stopped jangling.

If she hadn't been so rushed, she might have noticed some curious glances she was getting from her classmates. As it was, Persis concentrated ferociously on following the lesson and trying to keep her notes straight. Finals would be coming up next week. Between the piano recital she'd practiced so hard for and the hullaballoo surrounding Loni's wedding, she hadn't been hitting the books as hard as she might.

Now that she had her scholarship virtually in the bag—she suddenly remembered that fact and gave her teacher such a rapturous smile that he turned beet-red and dropped his chalk—she positively had to get decent enough grades so that she'd be graduated without a hitch next year. Besides, it was almost restful to fill her mind with English and math instead of the crises that had been dumped on her over this past disastrous weekend.

It wasn't till lunchtime that Persis realized she was being stalked by a posse of determined classmates. They closed in on her at the cafeteria.

"Hey, Persis," demanded Tiggy Tyes, who liked to think of herself as Persis Green's closest friend, "how come you never told me about Todd Ormsey?"

Persis had heard about people's hearts leaping into their mouths. She'd always thought of it as a figure of speech, until now. "What's to tell?" she managed to choke out.

"Don't give us that garbage. I saw you in his car yesterday."

That was Madeline Parks. It would be. Madeline never missed a fresh piece of gossip, or a moment in spreading it around.

"How long have you been going with him?" Tiggy was insisting.

Persis shrugged. "Ask Madeline. She knows more about it than I do."

How clever Loni had been to borrow that suede jacket and the distinctive matching cap yesterday. Anybody who mattered would know the outfit belonged to Persis Green because she'd worn it so much. With her light hair tucked up out of sight and those big dark glasses covering most of her face, Loni had banked on being mistaken for her sister at a distance. And she had been right. Terrific!

Persis was all set to straighten Madeline out when she remembered the Parkses were related to Chet's family. Tiggy Tyes was already furious because Madeline had been invited to the wedding with her parents, and she herself hadn't.

Loni had wailed, "If the Cowleses ever found out I was with Todd, they'd call off the wedding." They'd find out fast enough if Madeline got wind of the true story. Persis couldn't do that, not to her own sister. Not with that miserable diamond and ruby heart missing because she herself had given in to a moment of spiteful folly. What could she do, except what Loni would have done? Persis straightened her shoulders, looked Madeline square in the face, and lied.

"You don't miss a trick, do you, Madeline? I hate

to disappoint you, but it's really not much of a story. All that happened was that my folks took Chet and his folks to brunch at the country club yesterday. You probably heard about that. Anyway, Todd was there and came over to talk. He was making a big deal about this classic white Sting Ray he'd just got, trying to make Loni jealous because she'd thrown him over for Chet. So just for the heck of it, Loni and I thought we'd kind of string him along. He said something about going for a ride, meaning Loni, of course. She made believe she thought he was asking me and said sure, Persis would love to go. So he got stuck with taking me instead of her, that's all."

"Oh." Madeline was deflated. "Where did you go?"

"Just around. I didn't dare stay long. My mother doesn't know I went, and she'd kill me if she ever found out. She doesn't think Todd Ormsey is a suitable companion for a sweet young thing like me."

Tiggy laughed, like the loyal pal she was, but Madeline wasn't giving up yet.

"Then you weren't with him when he had the accident?"

"What accident?"

"Last night, out on Cemetery Road. His car flipped over."

"You're kidding! That's awful." Persis didn't have to pretend her concern. "Was he hurt?"

"Broken collarbone and a concussion. He was out like a light when the police found him. They took him to the hospital in an ambulance."

"How bad was the concussion?"

"They most likely don't know yet. You know how it is with head injuries."

Madeline made it sound pretty dire, but Persis could feel her knees buckling with relief. Then she'd done the right thing by reporting the accident, even if she didn't know whether it was her call the police had responded to or somebody else's. Todd might have been far worse off if he'd had to lie out there unconscious and untreated all night.

At least he hadn't burned up or bled to death. A broken collarbone wasn't so bad. She'd had one herself, after falling off her bike when she was a kid. And the jocks who played football and hockey were always getting concussed. Madeline always tried to make things sound worse than they were. But still—

"Madeline, I feel terrible," she said with total sincerity. "I suppose I ought to go and see how he's doing. He was feeling pretty depressed about Loni, and now smashing up the Sting Ray—that's really tough."

"Maybe this will bring him and Loni back together," said Tiggy with a sigh. She read a lot of paperback romances."

"Not a chance," Persis scoffed. "She's so hung up on Chet Cowles, you could faint."

This was for Madeline's benefit, needless to say. Madeline was quick to pick it up.

"She ought to be, after that gorgeous present Chet's grandmother gave her. Didn't you absolutely *die* over all those diamonds and rubies?"

"I wouldn't mind having that brooch." Persis was

going to add, "—to stick on my bicycle," but she managed to stop herself just in time.

"Who wouldn't? I suppose Loni's going to wear it at the wedding."

"Of course not," Tiggy took it upon herself to answer, dripping scorn at every pore for Madeline's ignorance. "Brides don't wear colored jewels. Just a string of matchless pearls," she added, switching appropriately to a dreamy coo.

Persis decided it would be a good idea to get off the subject of that brooch. "No kidding, Madeline," she said. "Was Todd actually unconscious when they found him?"

"That's what Jennifer Dunphy told me. Her brother's on the police force, and he was one of the men who answered the call. Jennifer gave me a lift to school this morning. She says they 'didn't know if Todd was unconscious from the concussion or if he'd just passed out from too much drink. They'll slap him with a nice, fat drunk driving charge when he comes to, I bet. Hey, you weren't drinking with him?"

"Madeline, you know my mother, right?"

"Sure."

"Then do you honestly think I'd be crazy enough to show up at the house with liquor on my breath, at a time like this? Anyway, I can't stand the stuff. You know I don't drink."

"Oh, right. You have to stay sober and clear-headed so you can devote yourself to your art."

Madeline found Persis and her piano an endless

source of amusement. Persis merely gave her a secret smirk, which, she knew, was the best way to get Madeline worried for fear she might be missing something.

"You don't know the half of it, Mad. Look, I've got to get to my next class. Thanks for letting me know about Todd. You coming, Tig?"

"If I must. Modern Dramatists, ugh!"

Tiggy crammed the last bite of fudge brownie into her mouth, dumped her tray in the cleanup bin, and followed her friend up the metal staircase. When they'd gotten far enough up so that Madeline couldn't possibly overhear, she asked, "Persis, was that true, what you said about you and Todd?"

"Tiggy, there isn't any me and Todd. It's exactly the way I said it was. He was making one last play for Loni. If you don't believe me, you can ask her. And Madeline was trying to make something out of a big nothing, as usual. But, Tig, I do have something important to tell you. It's still a secret. I haven't even told my parents yet, so you've got to promise you won't breathe a word to a soul."

That was enough to switch her friend off the ticklish subject of Todd Ormsey, as Persis had known it would be. Tiggy was perhaps a tiny bit disappointed that Persis's real secret involved nothing more romantic than a music scholarship, but loyalty prevailed. She squealed and burbled and did her best to achieve a proper level of hysteria.

"Persis, that's fabulous! Just what you've always wanted. And you aren't even a senior yet. I mean, most people don't even get to apply for scholarships before they're seniors. And you didn't have to apply. I mean, here's this handsome older man—" Tiggy wouldn't have known Frederick Lanscome if she fell over him, but that didn't matter. She no doubt had a clear mental picture of him already: lean, saturnine, and wearing riding breeches.

"And he takes one long look at you and becomes so fascinated by your—" Tiggy eyed Persis's new haircut sadly and had to amend her scenario. "—by your piano playing that he simply walks up to you and hands you the answer to your lifelong dream on a velvet cushion. Wait till I tell—oops, sorry! I won't even whisper it to my teddy bear. Not till you say it's okay or till I hear it from Madeline Parks, whichever comes first. By the way, are you really going to see Todd at the hospital?"

Persis managed a smile and a shrug. "Why not? That will give Madeline something else to talk about, won't it? I don't suppose they're letting him have visitors if he's got a concussion, but you don't have to let Madeline know I couldn't get into the room, do you?"

"Persis, you are something else! See you later."

They went to their separate classes, and the afternoon session began. Persis tried again to concentrate on her studies, but her mind kept wandering back to Todd Ormsey. It was some kind of luck that he'd been unconscious when the police got to him.

That was a rotten thing to be thinking, but it must have been fairly obvious he was in no real danger, or

Madeline would have had him already dead and buried by now. Maybe it hadn't been a real concussion, just that bottle of vodka. Loni'd said he was really drunk when she'd left him.

At least he hadn't been in a state to let the police know Loni had been with him. Maybe he still hadn't told anybody. Either way, though, she had to know. She'd been dragged too far into this mess to back out now.

Chapter 12

As Persis was leaving school after class, she had the luck to run into Jennifer Dunphy.

"Hi, Persis. Too bad about your boyfriend," was Jennifer's greeting.

Persis forced a smile. "Don't tell me you fell for Madeline's latest fairy tale. I thought policemen's sisters were supposed to get the facts before they jumped to conclusions."

"Madeline told me she saw you with him in that white 1967 Sting Ray yesterday."

"She did. So did a number of other people, I expect. Todd's family and mine belong to the same club, that's all. I ran into him when we were having brunch with my sister's in-laws. The ones who are going to be her in-laws after she gets married, I mean. Anyway, Todd was making a big deal about the Sting Ray, trying to make my sister sorry she's marrying Chet Cowles instead of hanging around for the rest of her life wondering if gorgeous Todd was going to call. But Loni wasn't playing, so he took me for a little ride instead. Then I came home, and that was that. Madeline's just doing another of her soap opera routines. Say, Jennifer, is it true he cracked up the Sting Ray last night, or was that only Madeline's next thrilling episode? She says your brother dragged him out of the wreck unconscious."

Jennifer, proudly aware of her connection with the forces of law and order, could be depended upon to tell the truth and nothing but the truth.

"It wasn't a wreck, exactly. The car flipped and landed on its roof, but it didn't appear to be badly damaged. My brother says what must have happened is that Todd parked on a side hill next to a gully and forgot to set his hand brake. The car got knocked out of park into neutral and started to roll. The wheels on the one side went down into the gully and the car turned over; but it was going so slowly, there was no real smashup."

"That's a relief," Persis told her, and meant it. "It's a fabulous car. How's Todd, do you know?"

"Sustained a simple fracture of the clavicle, which means a broken collarbone in case you didn't happen to know," Jennifer explained kindly, "and a mild concussion because he didn't have his seat belt fastened when he flipped, and let that be a lesson to us all. My brother says Todd was so drunk he didn't even know he was upside down when they took him out. You hadn't been drinking with him, by chance?"

"Neither by chance nor on purpose," Persis assured her. "We just rode around awhile, that's all. He was feeling down because Loni's getting married and wanted to talk. They used to see a lot of each other before she got engaged to Chet."

"Oh, so that's what started it. I'll tell my brother. And Fred will say, 'That's an explanation, but not an excuse.' You don't know what a strain it is, being related to the cops."

"You don't know what a strain it is having your sister get married. Want to swap? I've had about all I can take of Loni."

Jennifer shook her head. "Thanks, but I'll stick with what I've got. Fred's not so bad. I sure hope Todd Ormsey never gets in his way again, though. Fred's awfully down on drunk drivers."

"Is he arresting Todd on account of the accident?" Persis asked her, feeling the old panic rise again. "He can't do that, can he?"

"I don't think so, since Todd apparently wasn't actually driving the car when it turned over. They might get him for trespass in the cemetery, but that's only a fifty-dollar fine. They'll all be waiting to throw the book at him if he ever commits another offense in this town, though. If he's smart, he'll get rid of that white Sting Ray, while he's got a buyer, and buy himself something less easy to spot."

"Todd didn't mention he was planning to sell the Sting Ray."

"He probably doesn't even know he can. When they towed the car into the garage last night, the mechanic on duty told Fred he knows of some man who's anxious to get his hands on an early model like that one. Don't ask me why. I think they're ugly, myself. Anyway, it seems this man collects old cars and has pots of money, so I shouldn't be surprised if Todd could get top dollar from him."

"Really? That might cheer Todd up. He was telling me he'd bought the Sting Ray at a terrific bargain. I'll pass the word, if I get a chance. What's this collector's name?"

"I don't know, but Todd could call the station and ask Fred. Were you planning to see him?"

"If I don't, Madeline Parks will never forgive me. If I do, my mother will tear me apart bare-handed. I wish I'd never laid eyes on that Sting Ray!"

That, at least, was the unvarnished truth. Persis sighed.

"I suppose I'll have to. I'd feel like a crumb if I didn't. Do you think they're allowing visitors?"

"I should think likely. Fred didn't think Todd was badly hurt. He says drunks are usually so relaxed that they get off more easily than the other people involved. That's one reason he's so down on them. Oh, want to hear something funny? Fred told me it was some woman who called in to report the accident. She said she and her husband had been at the cemetery watching the baby owls hatch. Can you bear it?"

"You've got to be kidding!"

Persis laughed, as Jennifer expected her to. Inwardly she was thanking her stars that she'd insisted on making that phone call from the playground, and that she'd had that flash of inspiration about the baby owls.

"Well I'm glad it wasn't worse. I guess I'd better get over there, if I'm going."

"Can I give you a lift?" Jennifer offered. "My mother let me take her car today."

"Thanks, but then I'd have to come back here for my bike. The hospital's not far from where I live. See you tomorrow, Jennifer."

The ten-speed made quick work of the mile or so between the high school and the hospital. Persis rather enjoyed the brief ride, but she did get an attack of stage fright when she had to ask the woman at the reception desk which room Todd Ormsey was in. The receptionist didn't even look up at her, though, merely flipped through the card index, said, "Three fifteen. Take the elevator and turn left," and went on to the next inquirer.

Todd must be doing all right if they were letting visitors in. The woman hadn't even bothered to ask if she was a member of the family. Persis felt a shade less uneasy as she trudged along one of those interminable slippery-floored hospital corridors and at last managed to find the right room.

Todd was in bed with his arm in a sling, awake and bored. To her relief, he was also alone. She stepped over to his bedside.

"Hi Todd. How's it going?"

"Persis!" The patient was more surprised than delighted to see her. "What are you doing here? Did Loni send you? Why didn't she come herself? Hey, she's not badly hurt?"

"Why should she be?" Persis was cool enough now. "She wasn't with you. Don't you remember?"

"She wasn't? I thought she—ouch!" Todd had made the mistake of trying to raise his head. "Sorry, but that hurt. I have a slight concussion, they tell me. I honestly don't remember a thing about the accident, just waking up in this bed with an awful hangover. What happened to Loni? How come she wasn't there?"

"She must have decided to leave the party before it broke up. Anyway, the last I saw of her, she was safely asleep in her own bed. She probably doesn't even know about your accident yet. I didn't, till I heard it from your cousin Madeline."

Persis decided there was no sense in beating around the bush. Better say what she had to, and get out of here before somebody else came in.

"Look, Todd, I was talking with Madeline at school today. She said she'd seen me out with you in the Sting Ray yesterday and wanted to know how come. I couldn't let her know it was Loni."

"Why not?"

"Because that would have been total disaster, and you know it as well as I do. I told Madeline we'd bumped into each other at the club yesterday, and you'd invited me for a ride to try out the new car. I said we only stayed out a little while, then I went home and helped my mother clean up from a dinner party she gave Saturday night."

Which in fact she had done, in a manner of speaking.

"I said I didn't know where you'd gone after I left you, but I knew you were feeling pretty far down about Loni and Chet."

"Whatever gave you that idea?" Todd sounded annoyed.

"My feminine intuition. Anyway, it was the best thing I could think of at the moment. It might not be an excuse for your getting drunk by yourself in the cemetery and wrecking your car, but it's an explanation," Persis added with a mental thank-you note to Officer Fred Dunphy.

"I also told Madeline I didn't want it spread around that we were together because my mother thinks you're too old for me. So by now you can bet it's all over Donville that Todd Ormsey is dying of a broken heart, and if I were you, I'd leave it that way. You'll be surprised how many women are going to come rushing over here to heal it for you."

Todd's bruised lips managed to twist themselves into a grin. "Not bad, Persis. How come Madeline thought Loni was you?"

"Because Loni was wearing my clothes."

"Hunh!" He gave a little snort of laughter. "I might have known. You two are quite a pair, you know that? Which of you thought of the clothes? Loni, I'll bet. She always was full of cute tricks."

"Will you forget about Loni?"

"I might, under certain circumstances."

Todd was eyeing Persis Green as if he'd never seen her before. "So your mother thinks I'm too old for you?"

Persis smiled down at him and shook her head. "Forget it, Todd, it wouldn't work. You like 'em dumb and willing, they tell me."

The injured man was really laughing now. "Maybe I'm not too old to change my mind. I don't know if I'd be able to invite you for another ride in the Sting Ray, though. I'll have to find out first if there's anything left of it."

"The car doesn't seem to be badly damaged," Persis was able to tell him. "Jennifer Dunphy's brother was one of the policemen who took you out. He told her and she told me."

"Yeah? What else did he tell her? I'm surprised he hasn't already been up to arrest me for desecrating the cemetery or something. I suppose, from now on, every cop in town's going to be stopping me to find out if I've got Pepsi-Cola on my breath. I wish to God I'd never bought that damned car!"

"Then why don't you get rid of it?"

"How, for instance? Who's going to want a car that's been in a wreck?"

"I'll bet I could get you a buyer this afternoon."

"Some kid with three hundred dollars he's made slinging hamburgers, right?"

"Wrong. A wealthy collector who'd be willing to pay every nickel the Sting Ray is worth. And maybe a little more."

"What's his name?"

"I don't know," Persis admitted, "but I could find out. It's somebody Jennifer Dunphy's brother knows about."

"Her brother the cop? You've got to be kidding. Hey, how'd you like to put in a good word for me?"

"I can if you want. You might be doing yourself a favor, though, if you get in touch with him personally."

"Me?"

"Why not? All you have to do is call the police station and ask for Officer Fred Dunphy. You could thank him for coming to the rescue and tell him you've decided to get rid of the Sting Ray because it's too fast and sporty and you're going to get a nice, respectable old lady's car for a change. You know, hand him a line about how you've decided to reform. Maybe that will get the cops off your back for a while."

"That'll be the day, when I talk nice to a policeman. On the other hand, you may have a point there. Shake 'em up, give 'em something new to think about."

"It would be better than having them come roaring out at you the second you start to put your foot on the gas pedal, wouldn't it?"

"I don't know. That's one thing I've never tried, yet. Be a good kid and ask at the desk if I can have a phone in my room now, will you? They wouldn't let me when I woke up this morning, on account of the concussion."

"And I probably shouldn't have stayed here talking to you so long. You'd better get some rest now. I'll tell them on my way out, okay?"

"Thanks. Oh, Persis?"

She paused in the doorway. "Yes, Todd?"

"I don't suppose they'll keep me here more than another day or so. But if they do, will you come and visit me again?"

"If I can."

She hesitated a moment, then came back and stood looking down at him, her face sober.

"What happens if I can't?"

She wouldn't have believed Todd Ormsey could blush.

"What the hell do you think I am? Okay, Persis. We had a nice little Sunday afternoon drive in the Sting Ray, you and I. Then I took you home to Mama. Is that what you want?"

"You didn't take me home to Mama. She'd have blown a fuse if she'd seen us together. You let me off at the corner. Thanks, Todd. Take it easy. Stay away from fast-moving cars and quick-thinking women. See you around."

She gave him a warm smile and a light pat on his trussed-up shoulder, and went out.

So there was another bridge crossed. Now to get back to Loni and make sure she didn't ruin the good work by saying the wrong thing.

Knowing Loni, Persis wasn't too awfully worried about that. When it came to saving her own lovely neck, the future Mrs. Chet Cowles was not likely to make a mistake.

Chapter 13

"Where in heaven's name have you been? I've been waiting for hours."

"What for?" Persis was genuinely astonished when her mother met her at the door, looking almost distracted. "What's the matter?"

"I wanted to go into Lowrey. What kept you so long?"

"I had rehearsal."

That was a plausible enough excuse. Persis generally did have a rehearsal for one thing or another. "Why did you have to wait for me? Couldn't you just go?"

"I was afraid to leave Loni alone."

"Why? What's the matter with her?"

"I don't know. She's been in bed all day."

"Is she sick to her stomach?" Persis asked, thinking of the ruined suede jacket.

"No, but she won't eat anything. She says she isn't in pain, but she won't get up. She just lies there and sulks when I try to reason with her. She was supposed to go for her final fitting this morning and I had to call

112

up and cancel. Miss Liss is furious. Now I don't even know if she'll have the gown ready on time."

"Don't sweat it, Mama," Persis told her cynically. "If she doesn't deliver, she doesn't get paid, that's all."

"What do you mean, that's all?" her mother shrilled. "How can we have the wedding without the gown?"

"Miss Liss will get it done because she wants her money, that's what I meant. Why do you have to make such a big deal about every least little thing?"

"That's the thanks I get. If I didn't handle everything myself, how much do you think would get done around here?"

Persis wanted to say, "What makes you think any of it's worth doing?" but she didn't. She didn't think it would take much more pushing to send her mother straight over the brink. Muriel Green had lost weight during the past months, and she'd been too thin before. Her eyes wore too bright, her cheekbones too sharp under the tight-stretched skin, her voice getting shriller every day.

And for what? As far as Persis could see, the only one who really cared whether this wedding went off or not was Mrs. Green herself. And where was it going to get her in the long run? What was she going to do with herself after it was all over, when she didn't have her beautiful daughter Loni to lead around by the nose any more? Start hunting a husband for Persis? She'd be wasting her time on that one. Persis wasn't going to be around. Poor Mama.

They weren't an affectionate family as a rule, but Persis felt an impulse to put an arm around the taut shoulders and give her mother a squeeze.

"You're doing a great job, Mum. How'd you like me to make you a cup of tea or something?"

"Look out, you're mussing my hair," was all the thanks she got. "I won't have time enough to get it done again before the rehearsal dinner. Why couldn't you have told me you'd be so late?"

"I didn't think it mattered. You never said anything about going to Lowrey. What do you have to go today for?"

"I've got to find a duplicate for that brooch of Mrs. Cowles's, if you want to know."

Oh, God. She might have known.

"But you can't spend so much money," Persis protested to see what her mother would say. "Daddy's already squawking about how much the wedding's costing him."

"Don't remind me," her mother snapped. "I'm sick to death of hearing him rave about what we can't afford. This affair's got to be done right or we'll never be able to hold up our heads at the club again. I wasn't talking about real diamonds and rubies, silly. I thought I could try to find a piece of costume jewelry in the same design, or as close to it as possible. If I can't, I'll have to have one made up."

Persis didn't try to argue any more. She felt too sick. She only mumbled, "Go ahead, then. I'll go up and see how Loni's doing."

Before she was halfway upstairs, her mother was out the door and into her car. Persis dumped her books in her own room and went through into Loni's.

"Okay," she told the huddle among the pillows. "You can come out now."

"What?" Her sister stirred, then sat up, blinking from under touseled blonde curls. "Oh, Persis, it's you. Why can't you let a person get some rest?"

"You've had some rest. I wanted to thank you for ruining my reputation. It's all over school that I was out in the Sting Ray with Todd Ormsey yesterday afternoon."

"That *you* were?" Loni's drooping mouth began to curl upward. "That's a howl."

"I'm glad you think so," Persis growled. "Too bad you'll never be able to wear my suede jacket again. Neither will I, in case you're interested. Did you have to puke all over it?"

"Will you keep your voice down? What if Mama hears you?"

"She's gone to Lowrey."

"That's a relief. She's been up here every two minutes, pestering me about one thing or another till I was ready to scream. Persis, I'm sorry about that lovely jacket, honest. I tell you what. After I'm married, I'll make Chet buy you a new one."

"What if he doesn't want to?"

Loni's lovely hazel eyes widened. "He'll have to. I'll simply put it on my charge account, the way Mama does."

"What if he squawks when the bill comes in, the way Daddy does?"

"Let him squawk. He'll still have to pay, won't he? What's a husband for?"

"I've often wondered," said Persis. "Aren't you going to ask me about Todd?"

"Okay, I'm asking." Loni didn't sound as if she really wanted to know. "What happened to him?"

"Nothing too serious, thank God. Jennifer Dunphy's brother the fuzz got him out of the car after I'd reported the accident."

"Persis! They don't suspect it was you who called?"

"No, they fell for the owl-watching story. Jennifer says the guys at the station are still laughing about it. They thought I must be some kind of a nut. Anyway, she said the car just flipped over on its roof and wasn't badly damaged. Todd wound up with a broken collarbone and a mild concussion, but he didn't look too bad this afternoon."

"How do you know?"

"I went to see him, naturally."

"Are you crazy? What if Mama finds out?"

"She'll yell at me, which she does all the time anyway. Who cares? Lon, I had to go. In the first place, you put me in an awful position by dressing up in my clothes. And don't try to tell me you didn't do it on purpose to give yourself an alibi."

"Well, I had to do something, didn't I?"

"What you could have done was stay out of Todd

Ormsey's car. That never occurred to you, I don't suppose?"

"Why should it? You needn't start telling me what to do, like everybody else. I'm entitled to a little fun for—"

"Okay, Lon, let's not go into that routine again. I want to tell you the whole story so we don't get our wires crossed. And you'd better listen."

"I'm listening," her sister grumbled. "Go ahead."

"What happened was, Chet's cousin Madeline Parks saw you in the Sting Ray with Todd. Naturally she thought you were me because she recognized my cap and jacket and you had those big glasses all over your face. Likewise naturally, being Madeline, she started telling everybody she could get to listen. Today at lunchtime, she grabbed me in the cafeteria and asked me how come I'd started going around with Todd Ormsey."

"But you haven't."

"I know I haven't, and I told Madeline so. Tiggy was there, and some other kids, so I had to make it good. I explained how we'd met Todd at the club yesterday while we were having brunch with Chet and his family, which was true. I said Todd had been making a big play for you, trying to get Chet jealous because Todd was still mad about getting dropped, right?"

Loni shrugged. "Can I help it? So then what?"

"So I said Todd was talking about taking a ride in his new Sting Ray, and you and I thought we'd have a little fun with him, so you made believe you thought

117

he was asking me instead of you. After that, I said, he couldn't get out of taking me, so he drove me around for a while. Then he let me out and went off someplace by himself to pickle his broken heart."

"Did you have to say he'd been drinking?"

"No, I didn't have to. They already knew. Jennifer's brother said Todd was so out of it when they got him out of the car that they couldn't tell if he was unconscious from the concussion or from the liquor. Anyway, I had to say how sorry I was to hear it because Todd was really a nice guy and an old friend of the family and all that garbage. After that, there was no way I could get out of going over to the hospital to see him. It would have looked funny if I hadn't. So Madeline was convinced, I hope."

Loni shivered, even though it was warm in her bedroom. "She'd better be. That kid's a menace. Some great in-laws I'm getting!"

"Cheer up, Lon. They're getting you, don't forget."

"What's that supposed to mean? All right, Persis, I suppose you did the best you could. But what happens when Todd tells his side of the story?"

"Todd's not going to tell. He promised he wouldn't."

"How come?"

"Maybe he's crazy about me. Maybe he knows he'd sound like a jerk if he tried. Besides, I convinced him you weren't in the car with him when he had the accident."

"I wasn't."

"I know you weren't, but I made it sound as if you'd left sooner than you did. He admitted he was so drunk he couldn't remember anything about it, not even when the car tipped over, so he had to believe me. I explained about Madeline seeing you with him and telling everybody it was me."

"Oh, God! I know Mama's going to hear about that, one way or another."

"So what? We'll tell her we had to do something to convince Todd you weren't interested any more. We'll say we got together and pulled a switch on him because he wouldn't leave you alone and you were afraid he'd get you in wrong with Chet's family. She'd buy that, wouldn't she?"

"I hope so." Loni poked at her ruffled pillows. "What do you mean, maybe Todd's crazy about you? You're not his type. Besides, you're just a kid."

"I know. I told him so myself. Forget it, Lon."

"But why's he doing this for you?"

"Because I'm doing something for him."

"Persis, you're not—"

"Selling my virtue to save my darling sister's marriage? You've got to be kidding. Relax, Lon. All I'm doing is helping him sell the Sting Ray."

"But he just got it."

"Yeah, well, now he's decided he'd better get rid of it."

Loni slapped the pillows again. "I don't see why. It's a terrific car. Besides, what do you know about selling cars?"

119

"Nothing," Persis admitted cheerfully, "but I do know somebody is interested in Todd's Sting Ray."

"Who?"

"Quit making faces at me. Some man who collects vintage cars. I don't know his name. Jennifer's brother heard about him from the mechanic at the garage, last night when they towed it in. Actually, all I did was tell Todd to call the police station and ask for Fred Dunphy."

"Todd call the police station? That's a laugh."

"He seemed to think so. He was in a pretty good mood when I left him. So why don't you quit playing sick and get out of bed? You must be starved by now."

"I could eat," Loni admitted. "What's for dinner?"

"I don't know. Is Mary still around?"

"Go find out, can't you? Bring me up a Coke and some crackers or something. I've got to take a bath and shampoo my hair before Mama sees me and throws another fit. Where did you say she went?"

"I'm not sure, now that you mention it. She was sore at me for not coming straight home from school because she wanted to go into Lowrey."

"She still could. The stores there are all open Monday nights. But why didn't she go earlier?"

"She was afraid to leave you alone on your bed of pain."

"Oh, God! Will I be glad to get out of here. I'm so sick and tired of being fussed over, I could scream. Start the tub for me, like a good kid. Use the pink bubble bath. I can't stand that jasmine stuff Chet's mother gave me. It smells just like her. You can have it, if you want."

"You're all heart, Lon. Anything else you don't want to be fussed over about?"

"Don't be funny, just hand me my robe and slippers. Don't forget the juice and crackers. Did I say juice? Maybe a cup of tea and some hot toast would be better. Only hurry it up. And find out if Chet called. He's supposed to stop at Longyer's and pick up those satin pumps Mama took to be dyed for me. What was the big deal about her going to Lowrey?"

"She was going to try to find a piece of costume jewelry that looks like the bleeding heart brooch. If she can't find one, she's going to see about having a duplicate made."

Persis met her sister's eyes. The two of them stared at each other for a long moment, then Loni's face broke into one wide smile.

"What a relief! I might have known Mama would think of something. Well, what are you standing around for? Hurry up with that tea and toast, can't you? I've got things to do, even if you haven't."

Chapter 14

Persis shook her head. "I'm not going yet, Lon. You've got to tell me first. You took it, didn't you?"

"What do you mean?" With no makeup on and her hair uncombed, Loni wasn't such a convincing actress, after all. "I don't know what you're talking about."

"Oh, yes, you do. I'm talking about Granny Cowles's brooch that disappeared out of the living room. Why did you steal it?"

"Are you crazy? How could I steal it? It's already mine. She gave it to me. Anyway, I haven't got it."

Loni was crying again, not a bit pretty with her face so red and distorted. "Quit bothering me! Haven't I been through enough?"

Persis stood her ground. "Not yet, you haven't. Cut out the bawling, Lon. You're a grown woman now. Can't you realize what you're letting your family in for?"

"I did not take that brooch!"

Loni's denial was almost a scream. It was barely possible, Persis decided, that she was telling the truth.

Not all of it, though, she looked too guilty for that.

"Okay, but if you didn't, you know who did. Tell me."

Loni only stared at her, pale lips clamped tight shut.

"Come on, for God's sake. Tell me. Do you want to land us all in jail? Was it Mama?"

Loni shook her head.

"Then who? I'm not giving up, Lon."

Loni wiped her tear-smudged face on the ruffled white plissé blanket cover. "It was Chet," she choked out at last.

"Chet?" That was the last answer Persis had expected. "He couldn't have. Here, have a tissue. Blow your nose and talk straight."

After a while, Loni managed to get herself more or less under control. "It wasn't really stealing. The brooch is as much Chet's as mine. Daddy said so."

"But what would Chet want it for?"

"He's—he was trying to make some money."

"By selling his grandmother's jewelry?"

"No, on the stock market." Now that she'd confessed, Loni talked freely enough. "A friend of his gave him a hot tip. This stock was supposed to take off like a rocket, so Chet took some money he'd been saving and bought a bunch of shares. Only the stock went down instead of up."

"Oh, gosh."

"You can say that again. Chet's been sick about it. He doesn't dare tell his folks. Grandpa Cowles is always putting him down for being so stupid about business. He wanted so much to make a big killing and show them he knew how to handle money. Poor guy, I know just how he feels."

Loni dabbed her eyes with a tissue again. "And it isn't as if I'd wanted the brooch in the first place. I wouldn't be caught dead wearing a hideous thing like that, if I had my choice. Only it's so valuable, and that ghastly old Mrs. Cowles will be on my back if I don't. And I can't. Persis, what are we going to do if Mama can't find one like it?"

"I don't know, Loni, but Chet didn't take that brooch."

"How do you know?"

"Because he couldn't have. The brooch was still on the piano when he left. I know. I saw it."

"But Chet came back. Don't you remember? While we were out in the hall afterward. He ran in and said his grandfather had sent him to get something from the living room, then he went in there by himself. That must have been when he took it."

But he hadn't because it hadn't been until after Chet had left for good that Persis had hidden the brooch behind the sofa. Dared she tell Loni the truth?

Not if she valued her head, she didn't. Loni would tell her mother as soon as she could, and no matter who was actually guilty, Persis would be blamed for everything. Still, she couldn't let Chet be accused of something she knew he hadn't done.

"What makes you so sure?" she argued. "You didn't

see Chet take the brooch, did you?"

"How could I? I was already on my way upstairs when he came back."

"Okay, then you'll never convince me Chet took that brooch. He didn't go anywhere near the piano."

"But he must have. His grandfather'd been sitting on the sofa, and the piano's right next to it."

"What do you mean, next to it? There's at least eight feet between them. Loni, I saw what Chet did. I was standing right near the living room door. He just ran in and scooped the—I think it was a gold pencil—off the coffee table, and ran straight out again. He never got as far as the piano."

"Oh, Persis, are you sure?"

"Positive," Persis insisted. "Chet was in a big rush because the rest of the family were already out in the car, waiting for him. You remember that, don't you?"

"Yes, but I thought—it wouldn't have taken him a second, and he was so frantic about the money. Why didn't you tell me sooner?"

"How was I supposed to know what you were thinking? Nobody ever told me Chet had dropped a bundle on the market."

"You sound like Daddy, saying that. Persis, you're not going to tell him and Mama what Chet did?"

"Relax, I'm not going to tell them anything I don't have to. They've got troubles enough already."

"What troubles?"

"Well, for one thing, the brooch is still missing, isn't it?"

"Do you have to remind me? But at least I know now I'm not marrying a crook. Maybe that doesn't mean much to you, but it does to me. I was furious with Chet when I thought—"

"Was that why you made the date with Todd Ormsey?"

"I suppose so," Loni admitted. "Okay, it was a dumb thing to do, and I should have known better. Poor Chet, I feel as if I ought to make it up to him somehow. I know, I'll phone him at the office and tell him not to bother about the shoes. I can get them myself tomorrow."

"That's really decent of you, Lon."

Persis left her sister trying to work the dial on her baby-blue French phone without chipping her nail polish and went to get the tea and toast. Sooner or later, maybe, it would dawn on Loni that if Chet hadn't taken his grandmother's brooch, one of her own family must have.

Or would it? As long as Loni had a reasonable facsimile to show in front of Grandma Cowles and her other in-laws, she'd most likely be quite content to forget the whole sticky business. Unless Chet took another beating on the market and tried to pawn the brooch to make up what he'd lost.

Even then, Persis supposed, her sister could talk him into believing his grandmother had presented them with a fake. So why not simply go along with the deception and stop worrying?

Because it wouldn't work. If there was one thing

Persis had learned out of this bitter experience, it was that trickery was no solution. Once you started, every step led to another, and the farther you went, the worse it got.

What if Muriel Green did manage to find a substitute for the diamond and ruby heart? It wouldn't fool old Mrs. Cowles. She must surely know her own brooch when she saw it and would recognize a fake when she expected to see it and didn't. If Loni showed up wearing a replica, the old lady would no doubt insist on being shown the original to make sure it was still in the family. If the Greens couldn't produce the jewels, the question of the insurance would have to be brought up. Then they could hold the wedding in jail. Hunting the Lowrey boutiques for an imitation was a waste of time. Was Muriel Green so stupid she couldn't realize that? Or was she so desperate she didn't care?

Chapter 15

When Persis went to get Loni's tea and toast, she found a note on the kitchen table that read, "I fixed casserole and salad." Mary must be off at the roller skating rink with her boyfriend, making up for lost time. Lucky her! Persis turned on the burner under the kettle and slid a couple of slices of bread into the toaster.

It occurred to her that she was hungry, too. She'd been too harassed at school to eat any lunch, and it was a long time since breakfast. Mary's salad and casserole didn't sound like much of a dinner. What it meant was leftovers from Saturday night, no doubt, not particularly well disguised because Mary was not an inventive cook.

Anyway, it was food. Should she set the casserole in the oven now, Persis wondered. There was no telling when her mother would be home, and Loni certainly wouldn't exert herself to do it. She couldn't even be bothered to come downstairs and make her own toast. What would she and Chet live on after they were married? Take-out Chinese food and Kentucky fried chicken, most likely.

Well, that was their problem. Persis put a teabag into a fat little white china pot with pink rosebuds all over it, added boiling water, put the pot on a tray with its matching cup and saucer, buttered the toast so Loni wouldn't have to weary her dainty fingers holding the knife, and carried the tray upstairs.

"Here's your tea, Lon."

"I'm in here," still in the tub, sloshing around among the pink bubles. "Thanks, sis," Loni added with surprising gentleness. "You were sweet to take the trouble. Set it over here on the bath stool, will you? I'll do the same for you when you get married," she added with a giggle of surprise at her own words.

"That'll be the day."

Persis put the tray down on the white wickerwork stool and moved it over within her sister's reach. "I was wondering if I should start dinner. Mary left some stuff in the fridge."

"Anything good?" Loni took a bite of her toast.

"Looks to me like Saturday's dinner glopped up with cheese on top. You know Mary's casseroles."

"Ugh! I was thinking maybe I'd ask Chet to stay. You know, potluck with the family. But if it's only leftovers—"

"How potty does the luck have to be? If that's not good enough, why don't you cook something?"

"Me?"

"Sure, why not? What are you going to do after you get married?"

"Don't ask. I was hoping we could hire a maid.

Now that Chet's blown all his money on the stock market, though, I don't suppose we'll be able to afford one. Oh well, I'll manage somehow. People always do, don't they? Besides, husbands are expected to do their fair share of the housework nowadays."

"You going to do your fair share of his office work?"

"How could I?" Loni ate more toast. "He should be along any time now. Go on down and tell him to wait, like a good kid. I'll get him to take me out to dinner."

"What's he coming for, anyway? I thought you were going to let him out of picking up the shoes."

Loni smiled sweetly and reached for the last piece of toast. "I decided it wouldn't be fair to bother him at the office."

"Sure, Lon. I may as well go stick that casserole in the oven."

Persis was fiddling around the kitchen, snacking on fruit and cheese, debating about whether to set the table and if so for how many, when Chet rang the doorbell. He had a brown paper bag in his hand and a worried expression on his face.

"Hi, Persis, is Loni around? I hope I got the right shoes."

"You most likely did and it's no big deal if you didn't," she assured him. "Loni's upstairs getting ready to overwhelm you. Sit down a minute. Can I get you a drink or something?"

"Is Loni having one?"

"She just finished some tea and toast. She wasn't

feeling too well today."

"Gee, that's a shame. Nothing serious, I hope?"

"No, merely an anxiety attack over whether she'll ever be able to cook as well as your mother."

Chet, who sometimes appeared to be rather frightened of his future sister-in-law, managed a doubtful grin. "That won't be hard. All my mother ever does is warm up TV dinners on the maid's night out. My folks sure liked the meal your mother put on Saturday night."

"Did they really, darling?"

That was Loni, wafting down the stairs in a cloud of expensive perfume, wearing a pale green dress of some light, floaty material. She didn't have to be all in mauve tonight because she wasn't officially on duty as a bride-to-be.

"Oh, you got the shoes. You were sweet to do that. Isn't he sweet, Persis?"

"Sweeter than a lollipop," Persis conceded.

"I hope I got the right ones," Chet said again.

Greatly to his relief, he had. Loni modeled them, making a big production of wanting her bridegroom to approve her choice. In fact, the shoes had been her mother's choice, but that was beside the point.

Anyway, Chet approved. Persis had a hunch Chet would have been ready to commend Loni's taste if she'd stuck two paper bags on her feet instead of high-heeled satin pumps. Did he really have no mind whatsoever of his own, or was he still too upset over his financial fiasco to try using it again so soon?

"We were wondering if you'd like to take pot luck

with us tonight," she suggested in a spirit of scientific research.

Loni pouted. "Don't let her talk you into it, darling. It's only yucky old leftovers. I tell you what, let's go someplace cozy, just the two of us. Afterward, maybe we can stop at the drive-in."

Chet had brightened up at the suggestion of pot luck at home, but he obediently replied, "Sure, Loni, if you want to. Only I don't have much money on me."

"Don't worry about it, sweetie," she told him most uncharacteristically. "I've got twenty dollars Grandpa Dane gave me. Let me pay."

"You don't mean that."

"Of course I mean it, silly. You're always treating me, why shouldn't I treat you for a change?"

"But what would your folks think?"

"Who cares? We're practically married, aren't we? Married couples don't have to worry about what their parents think."

This aspect of the wedded state had obviously never occurred to Chet Cowles before. Persis wondered how soon he'd come to realize that doing as they pleased meant doing what suited Loni. Not before the honeymoon was over, she hoped.

Tonight, at least, Chet appeared happy enough to go off with Loni dancing along at his side, telling him how sweet he was. Maybe she was even coming to think so. That frightful episode with Todd Ormsey might have taught her to value her stodgy, predictable fiancé more highly. It would be nice if one positive thing came out of that mess.

Left alone, Persis went back to the kitchen to find out how the casserole was doing. Before she could get the oven door open, though, she was interrupted by the telephone. To her pleased surprise, Miss Folliott was calling.

"Persis, this is Angela. I don't know if you happened to notice in the TV guide that Frederick's most recent concert with the Philharmonic is being rebroadcast on Channel Two tonight at eight o' clock. I thought you might like to watch."

"Oh thanks! I'd love to. Miss—uh, Angela, do you really think he meant it about that scholarship?"

"My dear girl, I can assure you that when Frederick Lanscomo says something, he means it. He had to dash off to New York to see his agents about his next concert tour, but he told me he's planning to be in touch with your parents as soon as he gets back. It's a marvelous opportunity for you, I hope you realize that."

"Oh, I do. I still can't believe it, that's all."

"You'd better believe it. And for goodness' sake, keep up your practicing in the meantime. I'm giving you fair warning, they're going to work you a great deal harder than I ever did. But you're going to love it. Come and see me when you get a chance, and we'll talk. Now that I've lost you as a student, I want to keep you as a friend."

What a wonderful call! Persis was celebrating with

a further nibble of cheese when she got another. This was her mother, phoning from Lowrey.

"How's Loni?" was her greeting.

"She's okay," said Persis. "She went out with Chet."

"What do you mean, she went out? She's been in bed all day."

"I know. She got up."

"But why? She was sick."

"She wasn't sick, just suffering from an overdose of in-laws."

"I wish you'd stop trying to be funny. Did she eat anything?"

"I made her tea and toast. And they're going to dinner."

"What dinner? I never heard about any dinner?"

"It's not that kind of dinner. They're only going someplace by themselves."

"What for?"

"Because they felt like it, I guess. Mama, they're engaged, remember?"

All Mrs. Green replied was, "Where's your father?"

"At the office, I suppose. He hasn't come home yet."

"Then who's there?"

"Just me. Mary took off."

"I know, I said she could. Did she leave anything for dinner?"

"A lousy casserole and some salad. Will you be home?"

"No, I'll grab a bite somewhere. I have too much to do here. Fix whatever Mary left for yourself and your father. Just put the casserole in the oven."

"It's already in."

"Oh. Don't let it burn. I suppose Chet forgot to bring Loni's satin pumps."

"No, he got them, and they're perfect."

"Who says so?"

"Loni."

"H'mph. Well, all right. I'll look at them in the morning."

"When will you be home?"

"When I get there. If I don't drop in my tracks first."

On that happy note, Muriel Green hung up. Persis set the table for two in the breakfast nook, then sat down in front of the television to wait for her father.

Chapter 16

Dinner was not going to be a jolly meal, Persis knew that as soon as her father came through the front door. If there'd been anything kickable in his way, he'd have bowled it into the next room. He flung his attaché case on the table in the hall, hung his suit jacket on the newel post despite all the lectures he'd had from his wife about leaving his clothes around the house, and growled, "Where's your mother?"

"In Lowrey," Persis told him. "She just called."

"What's she doing there?"

"Shopping. The stores are open tonight."

"Ugh. When's she coming back?"

"After they close, I should think."

"Then what are we supposed to do about dinner?"

"Mary left a casserole."

"Great! A man slaves his guts out all day and comes home to a bowl of dog food. Get me some ice, will you?"

He was heading for the bar in the dining room. While he mixed himself a drink, Persis filled the ice bucket and got him a plate of crackers and cheese, along with a soft drink for herself. When she got back with the tray, he was in his easy chair by the television set. She gave him the ice and the snack, then pulled up a hassock beside him.

"Aren't you going to fix the food?" he growled when she sat down.

"It's all fixed," she told him. "We can eat any time you want."

"Then set the table, can't you?"

"I did, in the breakfast nook."

"What's the matter with the dining room?"

"Well, it's only the two of us."

"And I'm not worth the effort, is that it? I'm only the guy who foots the bills."

"Daddy, you don't have to bite my head off. I just thought—"

"You think too damn much, if you ask me." He gulped down his drink in two swallows and handed her the empty glass.

"Do you want a refill?" she asked.

"If you can spare the time from more important matters."

Fuming, Persis carried the glass back to the bar. She wasn't sure how much to put in so she decided she'd better err on the side of generosity. At least then he wouldn't be able to yell at her for thinking the one who paid for the whiskey wasn't good enough to drink it. Why couldn't adults manage to act like grown-ups once in a while?

She handed him the full glass. He took a sip, and choked.

"Oof! You didn't stint on the booze, did you?"

Persis shruged. "You bought it. You might as well enjoy it."

"Always got an answer, haven't you?"

He took a more careful sip, set the glass on the end table beside his chair, and watched the news in silence for a few minutes. When the commercial break came, he asked, "What's so important in Lowrey? I thought your mother'd bought out all the stores by now."

"She's trying to find a duplicate for that brooch."

"What? Is she out of her mind? Does she think I'm made of money?"

"Calm down, Daddy," Persis urged. "She's not looking for a real one, just a fake copy, in case she has to show it to somebody."

"But I've already—" Charles Green didn't finish what he'd started to say. Instead, he began furiously hunting around the floor beside his chair. "Where in hell did I leave that *Wall Street Journal?*"

"In your attaché case, maybe?" Persis suggested. "I'll go take a look."

Her father leaped out of the chair. "Don't you dare touch that case! I'll get it myself. Fix me another drink, since you're being so damned helpful all of a sudden."

He didn't have to yell at her like that. First he complained about the drink she'd already made him, then he barely touched it, now he wanted another. What was the matter with him tonight, anyway? She took the glass out to the kitchen, added a couple more ice cubes to make it look full, and brought it back. Her father was back in the recliner now with the paper in his hand and, she was surprised to notice, the attaché case in his lap. Did he think she was going to steal it or something?

Persis was getting hungry. Even that casserole smelled pretty good to her by now. She ate some of the cheese and crackers she'd fixed for her father, wishing he'd put down his newspaper and come to the table. He didn't even appear to be reading, just scowling at the pages and rattling them over and slapping them flat with the back of his hand, as if he hated the *Wall Street Journal* and everything in it. After a while, Persis decided she'd rather be yelled at than ignored like this.

"I don't know why Mama thinks a hunk of costume jewelry would ever fool anybody."

"How do you know it wouldn't?" her father yelled back. "You're so damned smart. If you'd only left that brooch on the piano where she put it in the first place—"

The attaché case thumped to the floor. Charles Green didn't seem to notice it. He was on his feet now. So was Persis, facing him, feeling the blood flame up into her face.

"How do you know what I did? Daddy, you saw me hide it."

"Think I'm blind?" He was trying to bluster, but it didn't come out very rough. Persis said what she had to.

"Then you're the one who took it out from behind

the sofa. You've had the brooch all the time. Daddy, what did you do it for?"

He didn't answer, just slumped back into his chair and buried his face in his hands. Persis knelt on the floor beside him, clutching at his shoulder, needing somehow to prove he was still with her.

"Daddy, what's the matter? Why did you do it?"

"What do you think? I've told her over and over. I just can't make her listen."

So that was it. All the complaints, the bickering, the yelling matches. Ever since Loni had broken the news that she and Chet were going to be married, they'd all revolved around the same thing.

"You mean you really can't afford it. You don't have enough money to pay for the wedding."

"That's the story, Miss Genius. I can't pay for the churchful of flowers, the two hundred roast beef dinners at the reception, the goddamned fancy favors on the tables, that ninety-dollar dress you tore to pieces—"

He choked and couldn't go on.

"So you were planning to sell the real jewels and substitute a copy, and nobody was ever supposed to know the difference."

"Go on, say it. Your old man's a thief. Satisfied?"

"Should I be? Daddy, you haven't already sold the brooch?"

"How can I? The copy won't be ready till next week."

"Then where is it now?"

"In my attaché case, if you want to know. And the

key's in my pants pocket, and it's damn well going to stay there. And you're going to keep your mouth shut about it. Look, Persis." He wasn't belligerent now. He was pleading with her. "It's for you as much as Loni. I've still got to send you to college."

"No, you don't."

"The hell I don't. You deserve the same chance your sister had. Maybe I'm not the world's greatest father, but you're still my kid."

He groped for the glass Persis was still holding and took another swallow. "Not that I haven't spent plenty on you already. Do you realize what those damned piano lessons have cost me, all these years?"

At last Persis had an opening. "Okay, Dad, you've spent plenty. But at least that investment's starting to pay off."

"How, for instance?"

"For instance, you won't have to send me to college. The piano lessons are going to pay for that."

"What do you mean?"

"Frederick Lanscome's giving me a scholarship to his Master Class School."

"Master Class School? What's that? Some phony diploma mill in East Overshoe?"

"Daddy, don't tell me you've never heard of Frederick Lanscome? He's a famous concert pianist. He plays all over the world."

"So?"

"So he came to my recital, for God's sake! You and Mama couldn't be bothered, but Frederick Lanscome came on purpose to hear me play. And if you don't believe me, call up Angela Folliott and ask her."

Charles Green was staring at her. "No kidding? How did he know about you?"

"He's a friend of Miss Folliott's. Besides, he judged the interscholastic competitions last month, when I won the gold medal."

"You did what?"

"I won the gold medal," Persis repeated. "And I can prove it. Wait a second, I'll show it to you."

"I'd like to see it." Charles Green sounded numb.

He was still sitting crouched forward, looking dazed, when Persis came down from her room with the little black velvet case in her hand.

"Here it is, Dad. It's probably only plated."

"Don't worry, I won't try to steal it."

He picked up the shining disc by its bright red ribbon and fished out his reading glasses. "First prize, for exceptional merit. Say, Puss, that's terrific. Why didn't you tell me?"

Persis shrugged. "I didn't think you were interested."

"Are you kidding? A gold medal, just like in the Olympics. This is really something. Didn't you tell your mother, either?"

"Do you think I could get her to listen? All she can think about is getting Loni married off."

"Look who's telling who." Charles Green sighed, laid the medal back in its box, then reached over to take his daughter's hand.

"Look, Puss, I know you think I'm a jerk for letting your mother go hog-wild over this wedding the way she has. Okay, I should have put on the brakes before she let things get out of hand, but I figured what the hell? I mean, what else has she got?"

"I don't understand, Daddy."

"Well . . ." He was having problems finding the words. "See, here you are, sixteen years old and already winning prizes and scholarships and all that great stuff. A few years from now, maybe you'll be up on a big stage in London or Paris like this Lanscome guy. Everybody will be yelling and applauding and handing you up bunches of red roses at thirty bucks a dozen, and where's your mother going to be? Over at the club, playing bridge with the girls. And Loni's heading straight down the same road, and don't think she isn't. This wedding's probably the biggest thing that will ever happen to her. What was I supposed to do, take away their moment of glory?"

Persis had to think that one over for a while. At last, she was forced to agree. "No, I guess you couldn't. I hadn't thought of it that way."

"Ah, you're still a kid. You don't know what life's all about yet. What the hell, what am I, if it comes to that? Just another Joe Schmoe who busts his butt at the office all week and has nothing to look forward to but getting out on the golf course Saturday morning and maybe breaking a hundred if he gets lucky. When I die, who's even going to notice I'm gone?"

"Daddy, don't talk like that!"

"Why not? It's the truth."

"It is not. Okay, I've made a good start with my music. But could I be doing it if you hadn't been earning the money to pay for my lessons? You won this gold medal, just as much as I did."

Her father looked up at her. "Is that really how you see it, Puss?"

"That's how it is, Dad. Come on, what do you say we tackle that crummy casserole before it gets all dried up? Want me to serve in the dining room?"

"Why bother?" Charles Green was far from glum now. "If the kitchen's good enough for a big star like you, I guess it's good enough for her old man. Going to wear your medal to dinner?"

"Why not? Give us a touch of class." Persis fastened the small gold pin to the front of her jersey. "There, how's that? Oh, Miss Folliott called a while back. She says there's going to be a rebroadcast of one of Frederick Lanscome's concerts this evening on television. Want to watch it with me?"

"Sure, I'd be glad to. Say, Puss, I was thinking—" Charles Green hesitated.

"What, Dad?" she prompted.

"The thing is, I've been putting aside a sort of little private bank account for your education. It's up around eight grand now. If you're really positive about this scholarship—"

"Miss Folliott says it's definite. She says Mr. Lanscome's going to get in touch with you as soon as he gets back from New York and explain the details. It's what he calls a working scholarship. I don't just get a free ride, I have to do some accompanying and teach a few hours a week in their junior program to help pay my way."

"That doesn't sound unreasonable."

"No, it's an advantage because it'll count as professional experience when I'm ready to start out on my own. I may not be ready for London and Paris in five years' time, but at least I'll have made some contacts and should be able to get work. Mr. Lanscome's students usually do. So if you were thinking about spending that bank account to finance the wedding instead of selling Loni's brooch, I frankly wish you would."

"Are you sure, Puss? I saved the money for you."

"I know, and I appreciate it. But you meant it to finance my education, and you've already done that. I can take over from here. What you can do, though, is provide me with board and room and carfare while I'm going to the Master Class School. It's right over in Lowrey, and it doesn't have live-in facilities, so I was thinking I could stay at home and commute. Would that make you feel better about the money?"

"Lots better. You can have Loni's car to go back and forth in. If she puts up a squawk about parting with it, we'll let her two rich grandfathers buy her another one. They might as well put their money where their mouths are. God knows I've had to listen to enough talk about it."

"Daddy, that's wonderful! Will you take me practice driving so I can qualify for my license?"

"My pleasure, Puss. Now, if I could only think of some way to get that brooch back without starting another big free-for-all. . . ."

"Easiest thing in the world, Pop," she told him. "Let's have it."

"You're not going to pin it back on the sofa?"

"That wasn't such a smart idea, was it? No, I've got a better one. Maybe we ought to take care of it now, in case Mama's feet give out and she comes home early."

. "If you say so."

Charles Green was quite willing to hand over the responsibility. He unlocked the somewhat battle-scarred attaché case he'd been guarding so furiously a little while before and took out a small brown envelope "There it is, Puss. Ten thousand dollars' worth of headaches."

"And here it goes."

Persis lifted the lid of the baby grand, took the glittering bauble out of the envelope, and dropped it down among the strings. Then she reached in and nudged it with her finger until it disappeared from sight.

"Where did it go?" her father fretted. "I hope we won't have to take the piano apart to get it out."

"Oh, no. You could even see it if you looked hard enough."

"But how's it supposed to have got down there?"

"Don't you remember what happened Saturday night? As soon as they noticed the brooch wasn't on the tray where Mama had left it, she and Loni started throwing my music around, trying to find it. Our story is that it got knocked off the tray and mixed in with the music, just as they'd thought. If they'd searched carefully instead of flapping around like a couple of windmills, they'd no doubt have found it right away, instead of letting it fall down inside where it couldn't be seen."

"And it's all their fault for giving us a hard time? Puss, that's what's known in the trade as playing dirty pool."

But Charles Green was laughing his head off as he followed his daughter out to the breakfast nook.

Chapter 17

The casserole was no more appetizing than Persis had expected it would be, but she couldn't have said when she'd ever enjoyed a meal in her own home more. Her father was interested in everything she had to say, or at least willing to pretend he was. He kept asking questions about her playing; some of them two and three times, but Persis didn't mind repeating her answers.

They finished their scratch meal with ice cream out of the freezer and cookies from a box Mary had tried to hide behind the cornflakes, then went back to the family room. At eight o'clock, Persis switched to Channel Two for the concert broadcast. Charles Green tilted back in his easy chair and shut his eyes.

"I can concentrate on the music better this way," he explained.

"Sure, Dad," Persis replied. "I'll wake you up when Mr. Lanscome comes on."

He only smiled and kept his eyes shut until Persis

prodded him.

"Here it is, Pop, the sweet sound of money."

"Pretty funny, aren't you?"

He sat up straight, though, and gave his full attention to the television screen when Frederick Lanscome walked on stage. The pianist didn't look fattish and baldish in his white tie and tails, with the black-suited orchestra massed around him and the applauding audience in front, and the splendor of the vast concert hall above and beyond them all. He looked magnificent. Persis felt shivery.

"Make believe that's me up there, Daddy, wearing my red gown and that gorgeous gold locket Gran Green gave me for winning the medal. I'm going to wear it for luck from now on, every time I perform."

"Rather have your grandmother's locket than a diamond brooch, would you?"

"Much rather. I'm off diamonds for life. Sh-h!"

Frederick Lanscome sat down at the piano, flipped the tails of his coat back across the bench as he'd done that night on the empty stage at the Community Arts Auditorium. He looked up at the conductor, waiting for his signal. Then he was off, darting in and out among the woodwinds, sending a cascade of notes over the violins, a crashing of chords above the horns, letting those magical hands fall quietly into his lap until the conductor's baton told him to pick up his next cue.

What must it be like to play with so superb an orchestra? Would she ever make it? Why not? Right now, this minute, everything seemed possible Persis forgot to notice whether her father was still awake and paying attention, forgot everything except the music and the man who was making it, the man who'd thought well enough of her musicianship to stand up and clap for her. She felt as if she'd been kicked in the ribs when a voice behind her shrilled, "Shut that thing off, for goodness' sake! How can you stand such a racket?"

"Quiet, Muriel!" That, of all persons, was Charles Green. "I want to hear Persis's teacher."

"What do you mean, Persis's teacher? Her teacher is Angela Folliott, who happens to be a woman, in case you can't tell the difference."

"Not any more. Sit down and listen."

Muriel Green was so astonished that she actually did sit down, for about half a minute. Then she couldn't stay quiet any longer.

"Charles, whatever are you talking about?"

"That guy up there, the one playing the piano. He's giving Puss a scholarship because she won the gold medal. She's going to study at his Master Class School. Right, Puss?"

After that, there was no hope of hearing any more of the glorious music. Muriel Green's high-pitched voice easily topped the woodwinds, the brasses, even the tympani. She had to ask a million questions, to examine the gold medal fore and aft, to wail over and over, "Why didn't you tell me the recital was so important? I'd have stayed."

"I didn't know it was until after it was over," Persis told her mother. "Anyway," she added cruelly, "it's just as well you didn't get to meet Mr. Lanscome that night. He was furious with you."

"With me?" Mrs. Green shrank back, as if Persis had threatened to hit her. "What did I do?"

"Made me cut my hair. He says I've got to let it grow back."

"But Miss Liss insisted! Didn't you explain to him about the maid-of-honor gown?"

"He says my career's more important."

A sustained fortissimo of applause dragged Muriel Green's attention back to the television screen. Frederick Lanscome was taking his bow, shaking hands with the conductor and the concert master, walking off, being called back to a standing ovation.

"They gave me an ovation at the recital," Persis told her parents complacently. "After my concerto. And Mr. Lanscome stood up and clapped with the rest of them."

"No kidding!" her father exclaimed.

"I suppose he felt he had to be polite," said Muriel Green. She still wasn't ready to accept all this.

"It was pretty damn polite of him to offer Puss that scholarship, if you ask me," her husband retorted. "When did you say we were going to meet him, Puss?"

"As soon as he gets back from seeing his agents in New York, Dad. Around the end of the week, I guess. He wants to get everything settled so that I can enter the summer program the first week in July. After that's over, I start classes with the junior program once a week."

"But what about Miss Folliott?" her mother demanded.

"Oh, she and I are all through, as far as my lessons are concerned. From now on, we're just friends."

Muriel Green sniffed. "Naturally she'll cling to you like a leech, hoping you'll give her an in with Mr. Lanscome. You'd better watch your step."

"Mama, Miss Folliott doesn't need anything from me. She and Mr. Lanscome are old friends. We all three went out for pizza that night after the recital, and they were going someplace after they dropped me off."

"You never told me he took you out to eat."

"You never gave me a chance. You were too busy tearing me apart for having to take the sleeves out of that stupid dress. You should have realized they were too tight to play in."

"That's right, Muriel," said Charles Green. "You've got to remember a performing artist has special needs."

"What do you know about peforming artists?" she snapped back.

"Not much, but I guess I'm going to have to learn. How about it, Puss?" He gave his daughter a fast wink. "Care to give us a sample of how you wowed 'em at the recital?"

"Sure," she told him. "I'll play you my overture."

All innocence, Persis sat down at the piano and launched into "The Whiffenpoof Song." After a few bars, she stopped short. "What's wrong with this piano all of a sudden?"

"It sounds perfectly all right to me," said her mother.

It did to Persis, too, but she wasn't about to say so. She played the passage again. "Hear that, Daddy?"

"Yes, I hear it," he obliged her by agreeing. "Sort of a—like a funny little ting."

"What ting? I don't hear any ting," Mrs. Green insisted.

"That's okay, Mama," Persis told her kindly. "You'll develop an ear when you get into it more. You just have to train yourself by listening quietly. Daddy, could you bring me a flashlight?"

"Sure, Puss. Just a second."

While her father was gone, Persis fussed around the piano, propping up the lid as far as it would go, trilling up and down the keys, striking one note, then another, saying, "Hear that?" every so often, finally getting her mother to reply, "Oh yes, now I hear it. Sort of a funny little ting."

Her father came back with the flashlight, looking happier than she'd seen him for months. "Want me to hold it for you, Puss?"

"If you don't mind. Somewhere around E below Middle C, I think."

"Where's that?"

"Right here." Unhesitatingly, Persis put her finger on one of the strings. "See if you can rake the light sideways, so it'll shine in underneath."

"Can you see what's causing the ting?" Muriel Green was not to be left out.

"Stand back out of the light, Muriel," her husband told her. "Let Persis see what she's doing."

"Daddy, look!" Even though she'd known all along what she was going to see, Persis felt a great surge of relief when the dazzle of precious stones caught the flashlight's beam. "There it is."

"There what is?" her mother demanded.

"See for yourself."

Persis stepped aside. Mrs. Green stuck her head under the propped-up lid of the baby grand.

"Charles! Charles, it's the brooch! I can't believe it. How did it ever get down there?"

Her husband shrugged. "Don't ask me. Seems as if I remember seeing you and Loni over here Saturday night, throwing Persis's music around. Maybe the brooch got tucked inside the pages or something, and you knocked it between the piano strings without noticing."

"That's right, blame me. If you're so sharp, why couldn't you have thought to get that flashlight and look in here before? Persis, didn't you hear that ting when you were practicing?"

"Mama, I haven't had time to practice. Yesterday I didn't dare touch the piano, because you had that awful headache. This afternoon I didn't get a chance because I was helping Loni pull herself together, then I had to fix dinner for Daddy," Persis replied in a suitably injured tone. "If you'll get me a ruler or something, I'm quite sure I can poke the brooch out where we can get at it."

"All that walking for nothing." Her mother was sighing. "I must have gone into every jewelry store in Lowrey and couldn't find a thing. And here it was, practically in plain sight all the time."

"Maybe that'll teach you to stay out of stores," her husband told her, coming over to the piano with a paper knife out of his desk. "How's this, Puss?"

"Perfect. Slim enough to—ah, here we go. Let me just give it another little scoot. Mama, your hands are the thinnest, reach in and pick it up."

"I'm almost afraid to touch it," Muriel Green said with unusual humility.

But she did. Half a second later, she was holding the ruby and diamond heart up to the lamplight.

"I hope to heavens Mama never finds out about this. I'd never hear the end of it. You know, Charles, now that I get a good look at this brooch, I must say I don't think much of Mrs. Cowles's taste. I'll bet she gave it to Loni simply because she didn't care for it herself. Honestly, I almost wish she hadn't bothered."

"You and me both." Her husband sighed. "Why don't you ask her to take it back?"

"Charles, we can't do that. She'd be mortally offended."

"Who cares? We're too highbrow for the Cowleses, anyway. Parents of a famous piano player!"

"Daddy, I'm not famous yet, or anywhere near it," Persis protested, though not very hard.

"What are you talking about, Puss? You won the gold medal, didn't you?"

"Sure, in a state-wide competition. That gives me forty-nine other winners I've still got to beat."

"I'm sure none of them got taken out to dinner by Frederick Lanson." Muriel Green sniffed. "Not that the Cowleses would even know who he is."

"It's Lanscome, Mama."

How sweet it was! No more put-downs, no more ridiculous clothes, no more having to play reluctant lady-in-waiting to Princess Loni, no more haircuts. Persis was on top now, and she was going to have her revenge. "I'd better write it down for you so you won't sound stupid when you meet him," she added kindly.

"Oh, heavens, what shall I wear? What shall I say? How am I going to manage? With the wedding so close and Mary acting so snippy if I ask her to do the least little thing—Charles, do you think he'd be offended if we simply asked him to dinner at the club?"

Persis stared at her mother in amazement. Mrs. Green's voice was shaky, her hands trembling, her face so pale you could have traced the outlines of her rouge with a pencil. She reminded Persis of—of what? Of those little kids Friday night at the recital, half paralyzed with stage fright because they were being made to step outside their small, familiar worlds and perform on a bigger stage, with strangers looking on and judging.

Persis knew all about stage fright. She'd had it herself often enough, but never like this. She'd always been well-enough prepared, on good enough terms with herself and her music to know she'd be able to do what was expected of her. Muriel Green wasn't sure. Maybe she'd never been sure. Maybe that was why she had to keep running around fussing and screaming, changing this, changing that, always having to be right, always insisting nobody could do anything but herself. Maybe she was scared to death that if she didn't keep up her act, people would find out she was really just one of the girls at the club.

Whatever Persis Green turned out to be, she'd never be that. She didn't need to punish her mother. Muriel Green was handling that job already. As gently as if she were talking to that shivering youngster who'd needed his shoelaces tied so he could walk to the piano without falling on his face, she said, "Don't worry about it, Mama. I expect Mr. Lanscome will be too busy to bother about dinner. He'll most likely want us to go over to Lowrey and meet him at the school. Afterward, if you want, we can get together with Gran Green and go out to a restaurant or something."

"Gran Green? Why does she have to get involved?"

"She's already involved," said Persis. "She's promised to put me up at the apartment any time I need to stay over. And I expect she'll be coming to concerts and stuff at school."

"That'll be fun for Mother," said Charles Green. "She'll get a kick out of representing the family."

"I can't see why she should be the one," huffed Muriel Green. Scared or not, she was no quitter. "Persis is my daughter, not hers. Now, Persis, about your hair.

I'm sorry that stupid Antoine made such a mess of it, truly I am. I knew I should have stayed and told him what to do. I'll have to scout around and find you a more reliable hairdresser. As for your wardrobe—"

Here we go again, thought Persis. It was pathetic, it was maddening, but what could you do? Stick her off at the club to play bridge with the girls? Persis glanced at her father and shrugged. Then she smiled. After a moment, he smiled back. She sat down at the piano and started belting out "The Wedding March" from Tannhauser.

"What's so funny?" her mother demanded. "What are you playing that piece now for?"

"Just trying to get back in the groove," Persis told her. "Hey, Pop, I don't know about you, but I'm still hungry from that lousy casserole. What do you say we go out for pizza?"